"What kind of husband did you have that you're so used to doing everything by yourself?"

Always a private person, Emily bristled at Slade's question. "That's none of your business. Just because we'll be sleeping under the same roof doesn't mean you'll be moving into my life." The feelings jumping inside her—the fluttery excitement that made her breath hitch and her mouth dry—scared her.

"Fair enough. We don't poke into each other's lives. Sounds good to me," Slade said.

Sighing, Emily sneaked a curious look at him. She hadn't meant it exactly that way. Now maybe he wouldn't tell her any more about himself.

She remembered that she'd had the first good night's sleep last night that she'd had in months. Was that because she knew Slade Coleburn was in her barn?

When was the last time having a man around made her feel safe?

Dear Reader,

March roars in in grand style at Silhouette Romance, as we continue to celebrate twenty years of publishing the best in contemporary category romance fiction. And the new millennium boasts several new miniseries and promotions... such as ROYALLY WED, a three-book spinoff of the cross-line series that concluded last month in Special Edition Arlene James launches the new limited series with A Royal Masquerade, featuring a romance between would-be enemies, in which appearances are definitely deceiving....

Susan Meier's adorable BREWSTER BABY BOOM series concludes this month with Oh, Babies! The last Brewster bachelor had best beware—but the warning may be too late! Karen Rose Smith graces the lineup with the story of a very pregnant single mom who finds Just the Man She Needed in her lonesome cowboy boarder whose plans had never included staying. The delightful Terry Essig will touch your heart and tickle your funny bone with The Baby Magnet, in which a hunky single dad discovers his toddler is more of an attraction than him—till he meets a woman who proves his ultimate distraction.

A confirmed bachelor finds himself the solution to the command: Callie, Get Your Groom as Julianna Morris unveils her new miniseries BRIDAL FEVER! And could love be What the Cowboy Prescribes... in Mary Starleigh's charming debut Romance novel?

Next month features a Joan Hohl/Kasey Michaels duet, and in coming months look for Diana Palmer, and much more. It's an exciting year for Silhouette Books, and we invite you to join the celebration!

Happy Reading!

Mary-Theresa Hussey

Mary-Theresa Hussey
Senior Editor

Please address questions and book requests to:
Silhouette Reader Service
U.S.: 3010 Walden Ave., P.O. Box 1325, Buffalo, NY 14269
Canadian: P.O. Box 609, Fort Erie, Ont. L2A 5X3

JUST THE MAN
SHE NEEDED

Karen Rose Smith

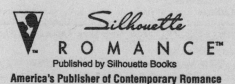

Silhouette

R O M A N C E™

Published by Silhouette Books

America's Publisher of Contemporary Romance

To Kevin Sharp,
whose music makes a difference in my life.
Meeting you was an exciting gift.

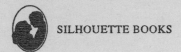 SILHOUETTE BOOKS

ISBN 0-373-19434-X

JUST THE MAN SHE NEEDED

Books by Karen Rose Smith

Silhouette Romance

*Adam's Vow #1075
*Always Daddy #1102
*Shane's Bride #1128
†Cowboy at the Wedding #1171
†Most Eligible Dad #1174
†A Groom and a Promise #1181
The Dad Who Saved Christmas #1267
‡Wealth, Power and a Proper Wife #1320
‡ Love, Honor and a Pregnant Bride #1326
‡Promises, Pumpkins and Prince Charming #1332
The Night Before Baby #1348
‡Wishes, Waltzes and a Storybook Wedding #1407
Just the Man She Needed #1434

Silhouette Special Edition

Abigail and Mistletoe #930
The Sheriff's Proposal #1074

*Darling Daddies
†The Best Men
‡ Do You Take This Stranger?

Previously published under the pseudonym Kari Sutherland

Silhouette Romance

Heartfire, Homefire #973

Silhouette Special Edition

Wish on the Moon #741

KAREN ROSE SMITH

lives in Pennsylvania with her husband of twenty-nine years. Wide-open spaces, horses and the mystique of cowboys inspire Karen Rose to write romances based on interludes spent on a farm as a child and basic values that last a lifetime. She believes in happily-ever-afters, and writing about them brings her great joy. A former teacher, she now writes romances full-time. She likes to hear from readers, and they can write to her at: P.O. Box 1545, Hanover, PA 17331.

IT'S OUR 20th ANNIVERSARY!
We'll be celebrating all year, continuing with these fabulous titles, on sale in March 2000.

Special Edition

#1309 Dylan and the Baby Doctor
Sherryl Woods

#1310 Found: His Perfect Wife
Marie Ferrarella

#1311 Cowboy's Caress
Victoria Pade

#1312 Millionaire's Instant Baby
Allison Leigh

#1313 The Marriage Promise
Sharon De Vita

#1314 Good Morning, Stranger
Laurie Campbell

Intimate Moments

#991 Get Lucky
Suzanne Brockmann

#992 A Ranching Man
Linda Turner

#993 Just a Wedding Away
Monica McLean

#994 Accidental Father
Lauren Nichols

#995 Saving Grace
RaeAnne Thayne

#996 The Long Hot Summer
Wendy Rosnau

Romance

#1432 A Royal Masquerade
Arlene James

#1433 Oh, Babies!
Susan Meier

#1434 Just the Man She Needed
Karen Rose Smith

#1435 The Baby Magnet
Terry Essig

#1436 Callie, Get Your Groom
Julianna Morris

#1437 What the Cowboy Prescribes...
Mary Starleigh

Desire

#1279 A Cowboy's Secret
Anne McAllister

#1280 The Doctor Wore Spurs
Leanne Banks

#1281 A Whole Lot of Love
Justine Davis

#1282 The Earl Takes a Bride
Kathryn Jensen

#1283 The Pregnant Virgin
Anne Eames

#1284 Marriage for Sale
Carol Devine

Chapter One

The mammoth, weathered barn with the floodlight on the peak of its roof beckoned to Slade Coleburn as snow swirled across his truck's windshield, falling heavier by the minute. The snow wasn't as much of a problem as his gas tank. He'd thought he'd have another chance to fill up. But the last stretch of road through western Montana had provided no opportunity for gas *or* food. He was now about an hour out of Billings and knew he wouldn't make it. Letting himself get stranded on a deserted road in a snowstorm would be absolutely stupid. Slade knew well how to take precautions for survival. The only sensible thing to do was to find shelter for the night—even if it was in a barn—then someone who could fill his truck's tank.

Noticing the small weatherworn sign hanging from a chain on a post by the mailbox, he read, Double Blaze Ranch. The short access road led to a two-story house with a front porch. The house looked as old as the barn, and as Slade parked and mounted the wooden steps, he guessed both could use some repair. Something to bargain with if he had to. He knew a lot about bargaining, too.

There was a doorbell, but it didn't work. When he opened the screen that should have been replaced by a storm door before this mid-November snow, he rapped sharply on the door. In a few moments it opened, but only a crack.

"Hi!" he began. "I'm going to run out of gas in another mile or so. I wondered if you had any to spare or an empty stall where I could bunk until morning."

"I don't have any gas," a soft, melodic woman's voice said. "Sorry."

He still couldn't see her, and he wondered if she was alone here. "Look, I know you probably have to be careful with strangers coming to your door, but if you want to get out a rolling pin and hold it over my head until I show you some ID, feel free."

The wind swept snow up onto the porch. It seemed like an hour until she finally opened the door a little farther. "Your ID's not going to do me much good if you want to rob the place or harm us."

"Miss—" he began.

"Mrs.," she corrected him. "Emily Lawrence."

He almost smiled because her good manners made her introduce herself even if he was a thief. "Mrs. Lawrence, I have references in my jacket pocket. I'd be glad to show those to you."

Suddenly she opened the door wide. "If you wanted to harm us, you could have done it while I was standing here. C'mon in and get warm."

When Slade stepped over the threshold, he saw a

beautiful young woman with shoulder-length, light brown hair and big brown eyes, who was very, *very* pregnant. "Now I see why you were so cautious."

As he took off his hat, he felt a tug on his parka's sleeve.

"Mom told me to be quiet and stay over in the corner."

Slade gazed down at a little boy who looked to be about seven. He had big brown eyes like his mom, but darker brown hair. Slade crouched down to the boy's level. "She was trying to keep you safe."

"She made cookies tonight. Want some?"

With a laugh, Slade straightened. "I won't take advantage of your mom having pity on a stranger. Like I said, I just need an empty stall where I can bunk for the night."

Emily Lawrence's hand lay protectively over her round belly as she glanced at her son and then back at Slade. She was wearing a denim jumper with a long-sleeved white sweater underneath. But the kitchen felt chilly, and he suspected that the fire in the woodstove over in the corner had burned down.

Looking around, he saw that the kitchen was clean, but the finish on the gray counter was chipped and the pine cupboards scratched and battered from years of use. From the looks of everything, along with his intuition that he'd honed to a high pitch ever since he'd had to fend for himself at the Cromwell Boys' Home in Tucson, he'd bet she used the woodstove as supplemental heat to keep her bills down. "I can chop wood for you if you need it. Or even pay you for the night."

"I can't take your money for letting you bunk in

a stall.'' She moved toward the counter and the cookie jar there. Even though she looked to be nine months pregnant, she moved gracefully. She was small and slender and he wondered how much of a burden carrying this baby was for her, and if she was married.

"Is your husband away?" It was the only thing he could figure.

After lifting the lid on the cookie jar, she studied him carefully for a moment. "I'm a widow."

Her answer surprised him. It had to have happened within the last year. Was she trying to run this place by herself? But though she'd answered his question, he didn't think she'd volunteer any more information easily.

Addressing her little boy, she motioned under the counter. "Mark, could you get the thermos out of the cupboard for me?"

"Sure." His smile was wide.

As he brought it to her, she told him, "Now go on up and get your pajamas on. It's time for bed."

"But, Mom…" He looked over at Slade.

She ruffled his brown hair. "Mr—" She stopped.

"Slade. Slade Coleburn."

"Mr. Coleburn is going to go out to the barn. There won't be anything here for you to see or hear. Now go get your pj's on."

With a resigned sigh that told Slade Mark usually obeyed his mother, the little boy went into the living room and then up the stairs.

Emily Lawrence poured water from the teakettle into the thermos, then added a few teaspoons of instant coffee. "I only have instant." Her tone was apologetic. "Would you like milk in this?"

"You don't have to give me anything," he said.

"When did you last eat?"

"Around noon."

"Well, it's almost nine. I have a few slices of beef if you'd like a sandwich to take along to the barn."

"That would be more than generous...and I take the coffee black."

Moving efficiently and quickly, she made him a sandwich and wrapped it in tinfoil. "Where are you headed?"

"Billings...at least for now."

She looked him over, from the cowboy hat in his hand down his parka, jeans and boots. "On business?" she asked.

He suspected she was still trying to make herself believe she hadn't made a mistake by letting him inside. "I'm looking for someone. But I'm also looking for work. I can do almost anything that needs to be done."

After she capped the thermos, she wrapped a few cookies in foil, too, then stacked them on top of the sandwich. "If you're hinting, I don't have any money to pay you."

"Room and board can be pay enough." When she didn't respond, he decided he'd better not push it and stuffed the cookies and sandwich into his pockets. As she handed him the thermos, their fingers brushed and, for a moment, neither of them moved. She was pregnant and wary, and his blood had no business rushing faster.

Her hand slid away from his. "Wait a minute, and I'll find you a blanket or two."

He hardly had time to put his hat on his head

when she was back with two wool blankets. "I really appreciate this," he said as he took them from her. "You didn't have to let me in. Why did you?"

After a thoughtful pause, she answered him. "I prayed when I heard you coming, and I used my sixth sense to size you up. Then I prayed again. My heart told me to open the door to you, so that's what I did."

Her answer wasn't at all what he'd expected. This beautiful widow with child definitely unsettled him. Going to the door, he stopped before he opened it. "I'll chop that wood for you in the morning." Then he shook a finger at her. "And don't open your door to any more strangers tonight."

When she smiled at him, Slade's whole world seemed to tilt a little. But he convinced himself he was just tired from a long drive. As he descended the porch steps into the swirling snow and made his way to the barn, he wondered what hand of fate had brought him here...and why.

Emily awakened before daylight the next morning, knowing something was different. Then she remembered. There was a man in her barn. A very tall man with dark brown hair, terrifically blue eyes, and a voice that smoothed through her like the brandy she'd once tried. The baby gave her a quick, hard kick and she smiled as she passed her hand over her belly. She'd had the first good night's sleep last night that she'd had in months. Was that because she knew Slade Coleburn was in her barn?

When was the last time having a man around made her feel safe?

When your daddy was alive, a voice inside of her answered.

The Double Blaze Ranch had been her father's and his father's before him. When she'd married Pete Lawrence, they'd moved in here with her dad. It wasn't until a few months had passed that she'd realized Pete had married her because he'd wanted somebody to take care of him. He'd worked beside her father on the ranch, but he did the minimum and only when he had to. Fresh out of high school, missing her mother who had died a few years before, Emily had wanted to extend her family and give her dad the grandchildren he'd always wanted. But she'd chosen poorly.

Thinking about her marriage to Pete still made her so sad.

The baby kicked again and she told herself she had no time for sadness. She had to be as prepared as she could possibly be before this baby was born. If there were complications, or the ranch was too much to handle after the baby came, she might have to sell it. She'd have no choice.

Never one to dawdle in bed in the morning, even during her pregnancies, she dressed in slacks and a roomy red top that she'd made herself and went into her little boy's room. Stooping over him, she murmured into his ear, "I'm going out to the barn to talk to Mr. Coleburn. But I'll be back shortly."

"I wanna come," he mumbled sleepily.

"Not right now. Try to sleep a little more until I come back in." Then she kissed him and went downstairs.

The coat that had seen her faithfully through the past six winters wouldn't button over her belly.

She'd be *so* glad when this baby was born. Three more weeks and she could see her feet again. After slipping on her boots, which were also a bit tight, she went outside and was instantly blinded by the sun shining on the fresh snow. Shading her eyes, Emily could see that her neighbor had plowed her road already. Everything looked pure, peaceful and white. She'd always felt that way about the ranch in the winter. Some ranchers dreaded it, and it *did* cause its problems, but she loved winter in Montana, even more than spring and summer and fall.

Larch and aspen swayed with the weight of the snow as she carefully passed a storage shed with snow mounded on its roof and crossed to the barn. She was careful about everything now. The baby made her that way...and she couldn't wait to welcome her son or daughter into the world.

Opening the small door on the side of the barn, she went inside. She loved the scents of the barn as well as the sights of the ranch—hay, horses, damp earth, the smells of everyday life that you couldn't find in town. Sunlight streamed in high dusty windows frosted with snow, creating beams and shadows, illuminating bits of hay and floats of dust. The snorting of a horse was all she heard until she became aware of a muffled sound outside at the far end of the barn. She knew exactly what that was.

As she passed an empty stall, she noticed the two blankets she'd given Slade Coleburn folded neatly in the corner. She fed the horses, patted them affectionately and did a few chores, then carefully opened the gate into the corral and followed the snow-covered cement path to the side of the barn.

Slade didn't see her because he was too intent on

splitting logs. But something must have alerted him to her presence because he stopped swinging and glanced over his shoulder. "Good morning."

"Good morning to you. I told you, you don't owe me anything."

"And I heard you. But I take generosity seriously."

Neighbors had been kind after Pete died, but she wouldn't accept charity. Looking at the log splitting as repayment protected her pride, and Slade Coleburn seemed intuitive enough to know it.

Noticing her open coat, he commented, "You shouldn't be out here. The temperature must be in the twenties."

"The animals have to be fed even when the temperature falls below zero."

His blue eyes held steadily to hers for a moment. "Do you intend to run this place yourself?"

"Until I decide what I'm going to do. I might have to sell." A real estate agent had been by a few months ago and had left his card.

A deep grunt came from Slade, but he didn't say anything more.

"Would you like some breakfast?" she asked. "I'm sure Mark is up by now. He wanted to come out here with me to see what you were doing."

"How old is he?"

"He's seven going on ten."

Slade laughed. "I wouldn't have minded, you know. He can watch if he wants."

Pete had preferred not having Mark around, said he was a bother, said he got in the way. "Have you been around children much?" she asked.

"Not since *I* was a kid." He didn't explain further.

A stiff breeze blew across the corral, whistling in the eaves of the barn. She rubbed her arms to keep herself warm. "So, should I set a place for you at breakfast?"

"Sure, but I guess I'll have to find something else to do for you if you do."

When she saw the amusement in his eyes, she smiled at the gentle teasing. How long had it been since a man had teased her? Pete wasn't that kind.

Before she thought too much about it or too kindly toward Slade, she headed back to the house.

Mark was waiting for her, asking a bunch of questions—"Was Mr. Coleburn cold in the barn last night? Was he going to stay? Did he know how to ride?"—one after another before she hardly had time to answer the first. Some she didn't have the answer to and she told Mark that. He could ask Mr. Coleburn himself. Then she'd really see whether the man had patience or not.

She'd scrambled eggs, set bacon to frying and warmed homemade bread in the oven by the time Slade came in.

"Smells great," he said. After he hung his hat on the rack near the door, his down parka joined it on the hook underneath.

Just as she was about to dish the scrambled eggs onto the plates, she glanced at him, and her hands stopped in midair. He was wearing a blue-plaid flannel shirt and jeans almost tight enough that she could see his thigh muscles. His shoulders were broad even without the parka. He was all man—dark good looks, ruggedly chiseled features and obvious physical strength. She told herself the sensation in her stomach was the baby moving, and the rush of heat to her cheeks she blamed on hormones.

Mark ran the same litany of questions he'd asked her past Slade. But Slade didn't seem to be bothered by it. He answered with "Nope," "Maybe" and "Yep" then he looked up at Emily as he pulled out a chair. "It looks to me as if you could use a few repairs—the house and the barn need to be weatherized for winter."

"I told you, I can't pay." She thumped his plate down in front of him, wondering why her heart was beating so fast, wondering why she was more conscious of him than she'd ever been conscious of anybody.

"And I told you, room and board would do it. I could handle the heavier chores. Certainly you can't do all of it up until the day you deliver."

"I can sure try. It hasn't been a problem up till now. Mark's a big help." After she put a plate at Mark's place and then hers, she sat across from Slade. "We say grace."

Slade gave a small shrug.

After a short thanksgiving for their food, she said to Mark, "You'll have to hurry a little or you're going to be late for the bus."

"What about checking out my references, then making your decision?" Slade pushed, continuing their conversation.

"Is work so hard to find?" she asked.

"When you don't know how long you're going to be in one place, it is."

From what he'd said, she'd gathered he was a wanderer. Why he wandered, she didn't know, and she knew she shouldn't ask. She was already feeling much too curious. "All right. I'll make the calls after I take Mark down to the bus stop. And before you offer, no you can't do it. It's just a little ritual he and I have. I need to see him on that bus and wave goodbye to him every morning."

Slade's expression suddenly looked pained.

There's a longing there, she thought, and wondered what had caused it. But whatever it was, it disappeared with his next forkful of eggs.

After she walked Mark to the bus stop, she mixed a batch of bread. She'd heard the fall of the ax as she'd walked up the snow-covered road and figured Slade Coleburn was going to cut her a very large stack of wood. She had to smile, thinking about his determination. She would appreciate the pile of wood when she had an infant she couldn't leave alone for any length of time.

The bread was rising when she made the phone calls to check Slade's references. There were three names and addresses—two in Idaho and one in Wyoming. One was a construction company; the other two were ranches. All three employers reiterated what she'd read in the letters he'd given her—Slade Coleburn was dependable, reliable, and stayed until he got the job done.

But then he moved on, she thought to herself.

In spite of her determination to get everything done that she'd planned, she became more tired as the morning wore on. Still, she made a pot of soup for lunch and baked the bread.

Slade came in around eleven when she was ladling out the soup. "Need help with that?" he asked.

"I'm fine."

"I guess you lifted that pot filled with water to the stove by yourself?"

She gave him a silencing look, but it didn't seem to affect him.

"You know, don't you, that pregnant women are supposed to take it easy?"

He was the voice of her conscience, making her think of her own good. So she made a decision. "I called your references. If you'd like, I can give you room and board for a list of chores and repairs. There's a small bedroom down that hall with a single bed. You can sleep there."

Coming to the sink, he washed his hands and dried them on the towel. She was standing at the stove, and he was much too close to her.

"What kind of husband did you have that you're so used to doing everything by yourself?"

Always a private person, she bristled. "That's none of your business. Just because we'll be sleeping under the same roof doesn't mean you'll be moving into my life." The feelings jumping inside her—the fluttery excitement that made her breath hitch and her mouth dry—scared her.

He didn't look upset by what she'd said. "Fair enough. We don't poke into each other's lives. Sounds good to me."

Sighing, she sneaked a cautious look at him. She hadn't meant it exactly that way. Now maybe he wouldn't tell her any more about himself. He reached for the bowls of soup at the same time she did, but she avoided touching him. "I'll get the bread," she murmured.

Slade spent the afternoon becoming familiar with

every aspect of the ranch. During lunch, he had learned Emily was due in three weeks. He'd also learned she ran about forty head of cattle. A neighbor had been dropping feed for her since her husband had died, but Emily had told Slade that she sent baked goods to the family every weekend in repayment. She was a stubborn little lady, but he had the irrational desire to know everything he could about her. As intensely private as she was, he knew that might not happen. He kept telling himself he couldn't be attracted to a pregnant woman almost ready to deliver. But that didn't stop the heat from surging to very particular parts when he was within a foot of her.

He was in the barn, cleaning out stalls when Mark came running in after school, slamming the barn door. "Mom said I can watch you, if you don't care."

Smiling at the boy, he shrugged. "I don't care. In fact, you can help if you want." He handed Mark a small shovel.

"Mom says you're gonna stay. How long?"

"I'm not sure about that yet."

"I'm gonna have a brother or sister soon."

"I know you are. Are you glad about that?"

"I guess so. I won't know till him or her is here."

Slade laughed, and the conversation continued like that until suppertime. Mark was open and inquisitive and quick, and Slade wondered again about the man who had been his father. But he wouldn't pump a child for information.

After supper Mark asked Slade if he'd play a board game with him.

"You don't have to." Emily's look at her son was tolerant.

"I don't have anything better to do, unless you want me to start weather stripping now," Slade responded with the quiet amusement Emily was coming to expect from him.

"I think tomorrow will be soon enough for that." She'd give him an hour. With Mark's constant questions, she predicted Slade would escape to his room as soon as he could.

The baby hadn't been active since early morning, and the aching in Emily's back had begun in the afternoon. She thought she might have strained some muscles when she'd lifted the heavy soup pot. The discomfort persisted throughout supper, and as she sat on the sofa and chose a marker for the game Mark had spread out on the coffee table, she plumped a pillow in back of her. With Mark chattering, there was no room for personal talk, and she was just as glad.

When nine o'clock rolled around, she urged Mark up the stairs, then read him a story as she usually did.

Her son asked, "Can Slade come up and say good-night?"

She hadn't anticipated that one. "You've already said good-night to him."

"I know, but it's not the same. Can he, please?"

She couldn't give her son much in material things, but she could give him love and affection and all the time he needed. Now, it seemed, he wanted time from someone else. "I'll go ask him, but he might have already turned in."

"Nah, he wouldn't go to bed before me."

She didn't think so, either, but she could hope.

As she went down the steps, the twinge in her back became sharper, and she continued to try to rub it away. It couldn't be the baby. She still had three weeks to go, and Mark had been a full ten days late. After she walked through the kitchen and down the short hall, past the half-bath, she stopped at Slade's door.

Knowing her son would be disappointed if she didn't ask Slade to go upstairs, she listened for movement inside, but didn't hear any. Finally she rapped softly. "Mr. Coleburn?"

There was a scuffling of boots, and then he opened the door. "Is something wrong?"

He'd rolled up his flannel shirtsleeves and unbuttoned the top two buttons of his shirt. Dark brown hair curled there. It was as dark as the beard shadow outlining his jaw. "No. Nothing's wrong. Mark just wondered if you would come up and say good-night. I know it's an imposition—"

"It's not an imposition to say good-night to a little boy. But you shouldn't be going up and down the steps so much, should you?"

"In moderation, exercise is good for a pregnant woman, Mr. Coleburn."

"Slade."

It was hard for her to say it aloud, though she'd called him by his first name in her thoughts. She knew if they were on a first-name basis, they'd breach the boundary of formality. But he was sharing meals with them, and he was going to say good-night to her son. "Slade," she repeated softly.

When he gave her a tilted smile, her heart jumped. Turning away from him, she headed back upstairs.

There were three rooms there—the larger bedroom, Mark's room, then a smaller room she had used for sewing that would soon be the nursery. Not so long ago, she'd painted Mark's light blue. He'd hung up a poster of his favorite baseball hero, as well as some school projects and a photograph of the horses. Every night before he went to bed, he picked up his toys, but the toy chest lid wasn't quite closed.

Slade followed her inside and stood beside the single pine bed, a twin to the one down in his room. "Your mom said you'd like to say good-night."

"Yeah, I would. Know any good stories you can tell me?"

"Mark..." she warned. "He's stalling," she said to Slade. "I already read him one of his favorite books."

"Maybe another night," Slade offered.

"Did you say your prayers?" Emily asked her son.

He nodded his head vigorously.

"All right, then. You sleep tight until morning." She gave him a huge hug and kissed his cheek.

Stepping closer to Mark, Slade made a pretend chuck under his chin. "See you tomorrow, pardner."

Mark's smile was wider than Emily had seen it in weeks. As she and Slade stood at the rail of the stairs, another twinge of pain sharply pierced her back. She tried to hide it, but Slade asked, "What's wrong?"

"Nothing."

"Are you sure?"

"I overdid it today. A good night's sleep is all I need."

"And you'll take it easy tomorrow?"

"We'll see," she said quietly. "Good night."

"Good night."

Even as she walked to her room, the huskiness of Slade's deep voice stayed with her. Readying herself for bed, she thought about how good a massage would feel, and then an unbidden picture of Slade—his large hands, a bottle of lotion in them—filled her mind. But before her imagination could take it any further, she put on her nightgown and slid into bed.

She'd hardly turned out the light when the pain in her back became sharper. With a sigh, she pushed herself up and managed to stand again, walking back and forth across the room a few times. The muscles were cramping, that was all. She would take it easy tomorrow.

But her pacing didn't help, and after a few more strolls across the room, the sharpest pain she'd ever felt twisted at the base of her spine as she fell to her knees. She couldn't get up again, and she knew Slade would never hear her if she tried to call. Reaching for the book she'd laid on the nightstand, she managed to grab it and pounded with it on the floor.

Chapter Two

Lounging on his bed, thinking about driving to the Billings courthouse the next day, Slade suddenly became alert when he heard a thump on the ceiling. Since he'd said good-night to Emily, he'd been elementally aware that she was in the room above him.

Had she dropped something?

Then he heard the pounding. It was strange, sort of methodical...three thumps, then another three. He didn't have to wait any longer to realize she was trying to send him a message. Instantly on his feet, he strode down the hall, then took the steps two at a time, faster than he could say jackrabbit. What he found when he reached Emily's room made his heart pound dangerously hard in his chest.

She was on the floor and looked terrified. "Labor," she gasped. "It didn't happen this way before."

He didn't know much about labor and childbirth,

but he could see that Emily was in distress. Crouching down beside her, he said, "Let me help you to the bed."

"I have to go to the hospital."

"Did this just start?"

She bit her lower lip. "I guess it's been building all day and I didn't know it. With Mark I just started having contractions about a half hour apart, then fifteen minutes apart, and it lasted about seven hours. This just started all at once—" As she said it, she gasped, and he could see that she was in pain.

"Emily, what can I do?"

As she panted, she held up her hand for a few moments. When the pain seemed to pass, she wiped her hand across her brow. "Can you take me to the hospital? I know this is a terrible imposition—"

"Hell, Emily. This isn't an imposition. It's a crisis!"

Gaining a bit of her composure back, she gave him a small smile. "It's just childbirth, Slade."

"Looks like a crisis to me," he muttered.

"We'll have to get Mark up. I'll try to make it downstairs."

Spunk was one thing, foolishness was another. "You'll do no such thing. I'll take you down, then I'll come back up here for Mark."

"Slade, I'm just having a baby…" But her words trailed off as another contraction swept over her.

"Yeah! And probably sooner than later. Don't you have an ambulance or something out here?"

"This is Montana. We can be halfway to Billings till the ambulance gets here."

He wasn't sure of that logic, but he wasn't going

to argue with her now. Before she understood what he was going to do, he scooped her up into his arms.

"Slade!" she protested.

"This is quicker, Emily. The last thing I need is you falling down the stairs."

"And what if we *both* fall?" she asked with raised brows.

He shook his head. "You're the most stubborn woman I've ever known."

"You've only known me a day."

"That tells you something, doesn't it?" he said with a hard look as he carried her to the top of the stairs, then down into the living room and deposited her on the sofa. "I'll be right back."

Returning to Mark's room, he awakened the boy and told him what was happening. It was just as well Mark knew the score.

"Is she okay?" the little boy asked.

"She will be. But we have to get her to the hospital in a hurry. Think you can get yourself dressed while I look after her?"

Mark's head bobbed.

Slade left Mark to it and went to take care of Emily. But, of course, she wasn't still on the sofa. He could tell she was going to be a bigger handful than Mark ever could be. When he found her, she was sitting on a kitchen chair with her coat on, trying to pull on one boot.

With a shake of his head, he went over to her. Taking the tall black boot from her, he held it while she slipped her foot into it.

"They're tight," she said, looking embarrassed.

"You're pregnant, Emily. I'd imagine everything is tight."

When she laughed, her laugh was as exciting as everything else about her. This was the first he'd heard it. By the time he'd helped her ease into the other boot, Mark had joined them in the kitchen, blinking sleep out of his eyes.

After Emily got to her feet, she took a set of keys from the windowsill over the sink. "I have a van parked in the bigger shed over by the barn. It doesn't look like much but it runs real well. And it has a full tank of gas," she added with a little smile.

The ranch and Emily Lawrence had filled his world for the day and he'd forgotten all about his almost-empty gas tank. "Don't move," he warned her, as he snatched his hat and coat from the rack and hurried out to the shed.

Slade seemed to work on autopilot as he carried Emily to the van amid her many protests, then made sure Mark was safely seated in the back. He tried to do everything quickly without panic so as not to alarm either of them. But he knew the danger of this trip to the hospital. Anything could happen when a baby was trying to be born. He just wanted to make sure Emily was safely in the care of competent doctors when it happened.

Twenty minutes down the road, Emily gasped, and it was a different sound than she'd made before.

"What is it?"

In a low murmur, she said, "My water broke and the pressure—"

His foot pushed down harder on the accelerator. But after another five minutes she doubled over in the seat.

"Emily?"

"I think I'm having this baby, Slade."

He could hardly make out her words. "Now?"

"Right now."

He swore, then clamped his lips shut as he remembered Mark in the back. Seeing a light farther up the road, he asked, "Can you give me five more minutes?"

"*I* can, but I don't know about the baby."

It was a cold night, probably only fifteen degrees, but he was sweating harder than if he'd been chopping wood in the sun in August.

As he zoomed down the road, Mark asked him, "Is Mom gonna be all right?" Tears quivered in the boy's voice.

"You bet. We're going to see to it." The light he'd seen was farther away than he'd guessed, and it wasn't on the road, but offset quite a ways.

Emily grasped his arm. "Slade, we've got to stop. I've got to—"

He told himself to keep his head. He told himself he could do whatever needed to be done. He told himself he'd take care of Emily Lawrence. Clicking on the flashers, he pulled over to the side of the road. "Mark, I'm going to need your help."

"What can *I* do?"

Looking directly at Mark, Slade was glad Emily had taught her boy how to listen. "You're going to sit in the driver's seat and lay on the horn. Three times…wait a bit…then three times again. You're just going to keep doing that no matter what else happens. Got it?"

"Okay," the seven-year-old murmured.

Jumping out of the van, Slade shrugged off his coat and hat, then opened the sliding door. Motioning Mark out, he saw the boy safely into the driver's seat. "Go ahead," he directed.

Mark laid on the horn once, then with more confidence did it again.

With a nod of approval, Slade went around for Emily. She was panting, breathing hard and fast, and doubled over. It seemed like a major feat for him to figure out how to remove the middle seat of the van, shuck it out onto the side of the road and get her into the back.

When he used his coat as a pillow for her head, she managed, "Blanket in the back—for the baby."

Taking her hand for a moment, he squeezed it. "It's going to be okay, Emily." He was going to do everything in his power to make sure of that.

There were two blankets in the back—one soft, one more coarse. There was also a small shovel, a jug of water, two candy bars rubber-banded to a flashlight and a bag of wood chips. Apparently Emily was prepared for getting stranded in the snow. He shook his head, amazed that such a slight little thing as she was reminded him of a pioneer woman crossing the Northwest.

Mark kept up the beeps on the horn as Slade covered Emily with the wool blanket. "How are we doing?" he asked her.

"I have to push, Slade. I don't know if I should. But I can't wait."

Not wanting to yell over the sounds of the horn, he tapped Mark on the shoulder. "Hold up a minute."

Then he looked down at her apologetically. "I'm going to have to look, Emily."

The light inside the van glowed down on her, and

he watched the expression on her face. "I know," she responded in a low voice. "Do whatever you have to do."

The first thing he did was pull off her boots, and then he made her as comfortable as he could. The idea of looking at her and touching her embarrassed him almost as much as it did her. But as he checked and saw the baby's head, he knew this was going to happen quickly.

"Slade?" She held her hand out to him. "Take this. You'll need it for the umbilical cord."

In the dim light, he saw that it was a pink satin ribbon. She must have torn it from her nightgown. "Mark, hit the horn again, longer and harder," he ordered, trying not to panic.

Her contractions were coming hard and fast, but now the baby didn't seem to want to be born. Slade hadn't prayed in years, but he sent a few words heavenward.

"A car's coming," Mark said.

Lights were headed toward them, and Slade didn't want to leave Emily. But he had to flag down that car.

As he scrambled out of the van, the oncoming car slowed, and a brawny man with a full beard wound down the window. "What's the problem?"

"She's having a baby. Get to a phone and call an ambulance fast."

"I've got a cell phone right here."

Slade wasn't much for modern conveniences, but right now he appreciated twentieth-century inventions. Returning to the back of the van, he thought about the best thing to do. "Emily, I'm going to prop you up a little bit. I think it'll make this easier, and then when the next contraction comes, push. Push like you've never pushed before. Okay?''

Climbing into the van, he put his arms around her to help prop her higher against the door. Even in these circumstances, he was so aware of everything about her, from the scent of her shampoo to the creaminess of her skin, to the determination in her brown eyes. He couldn't help but lean close to her, brush his hand down her cheek and say, ''We're going to do this, Emily.''

Her chin rested in his palm for a moment, and he saw tears gather in her eyes. Then she nodded and said, ''I'm ready.''

He hoped to heaven *he* was.

At her feet again, he waited for the next contraction. It swept her body, and she tensed. He didn't have to encourage her because she pushed with all her might. Suddenly he was holding her baby's head in his hands. ''Again, Emily. C'mon. Let's get it out.''

It seemed forever until the next contraction, but then it came, and Emily pushed and pushed and pushed, and he held a perfect little girl in his hands.

The moment choked his chest and tightened his throat, and he didn't imagine he could feel so deeply ever again. This was a miracle.

But then he moved and moved quickly, making sure the baby was breathing, tying off the cord, wrapping her in the blanket. When he laid the bundle in Emily's arms, he asked, ''Do you know her name?''

There were tears falling down Emily's cheeks, and she nodded. ''Amanda. I'm going to call her Amanda.''

When they were still lost in the wonder of what had happened, they heard the siren, and then Slade saw flashing lights. He moved out of the way, and a short time later held Mark's shoulder as the paramedics took care of Emily and the baby. Driving behind them to the hospital, he hoped he'd done everything right and that nothing would go wrong.

In the waiting room on the maternity floor, Mark finally fell asleep on the sofa, leaning against Slade's shoulder. He looked down at the little boy and felt a bit of the responsibility that Emily must feel every day.

When a nurse finally came to the waiting area, she said, "You can see your wife now if you'd like."

"Oh, but she's not..." He stopped. Maybe if he told the nurse the truth she wouldn't let him see Emily. "I hate to leave the boy here alone."

"I'll watch him. Go ahead. You shouldn't stay long anyway. She could use a good night's sleep after what she's been through."

Following the arrows, he found the room easily. There were two beds, but one was empty. As he stepped inside, he saw the baby in a portable carrier near Emily. Emily's eyes were closed, and he wondered if she'd already fallen asleep.

But then she opened them and looked up at him. "Quite a ride." She gave him a small smile.

Approaching the bed, he teased, "I don't want to do that again, anytime soon."

She laughed. "Me, either."

After he pulled a chair over to the side of the bed, he sat down for a moment. "Are you really okay?"

"I'm fine. Amanda's fine. But Slade—" She stopped. "Never mind."

"What?" he asked.

"I shouldn't have come here. There are going to be bills, and…"

For years he'd worked, only spending money on necessities. The rest had built into quite a nest egg. Maybe once she got to know him better, she'd accept some help. Nothing in this world could have kept his hand from covering hers. "Don't think about that now. You and the baby had to get checked out. It was the safe thing to do."

"I'm coming home tomorrow."

"Are you sure?" he asked.

"The doctor said if I take it easy, it's okay to go home."

"What time do you want me to be here?"

"Are you sure you want to get any more mixed up in this?" she asked solemnly.

"I'm already in it. What time?"

After a pause, she answered, "Around eleven?"

"No problem. I think my schedule's clear." He smiled, and then looked at the baby. "She's beautiful, Emily."

Emily nodded. "I know. Thank you, Slade."

His hand was still covering hers, and he suddenly wished he could hold it all night, wished that he could hold *her* all night. But that was crazy.

Leaning back in his chair, he pulled away, then stood. "I'll be here tomorrow morning. I'm going to go get Mark and bring him in to say good-night. I don't want him to worry about you, *or* Amanda."

"That's a good idea." Emily's smile was full of gratitude.

When he left Emily's room, he took a deep breath. It had been one hell of a night, and he was more than a little mixed up in it. Somehow he'd gotten much too involved. He should know better. Nothing lasted, and he wasn't sure it should. Not one thing had ever been stable in his life. At the boys' home, he'd make friends and then they'd leave. The staff had come and gone. When he'd left, it had seemed only natural to never stay in one place very long.

Besides that, he had a brother to find.

But as he went to fetch Mark, he knew no matter where he went or what he did, he'd always remember this night.

Forever.

As Slade suspected, Mark fell asleep on the way home. Slade woke him gently, and Mark sleepily crawled out of the van and grabbed for Slade's hand as they followed the walk to the door. Inside he went straight upstairs without even taking his coat off. Slade helped the seven-year-old into his pajamas, then tucked him in.

But Mark looked up at him. "Can you stay up here with me?"

"I might snore and keep you awake," he joked, not knowing if that was a good idea.

"Please?" Mark asked.

There was no way Slade could refuse him. "I'll tell you what. Why don't I sit here until you fall asleep. Then I'll stretch out in your mom's room."

Mark smiled at him, then snuggled into the pillow. Slade watched Emily's son as he slid easily into sleep. Pushing up from the bedroom chair, he quietly left Mark's room but kept the door ajar. At the threshold of Emily's bedroom, he stopped.

This was a *bad* idea. The room wasn't a frilly room, but it was feminine. A white ruffled duster ran around the bed, and what looked like a hand-sewn quilt in pink, blue and white, lay on top of the sheets. The covers were disturbed now, and he stepped closer, aware of the scent of roses. It was the same scent that seemed to cling to her. He saw the bottle of lotion on the nightstand.

It seemed an invasion of Emily's privacy to sleep in her bed, but he didn't want to disappoint Mark. So he straightened the sheets and smoothed out the quilt, lying on top of it. He noticed pictures of Mark on the small chest of drawers and a framed photo of an older man. But that photograph looked aged, and he suspected it might be Emily's father. There was another smaller photograph with the same man, his arm around a pretty young woman. That photograph, too, looked old—Emily's parents. Pictures of a younger man who might have been her husband were absent, and Slade wondered why.

A pale blue chenille robe hung on an old-fashioned clothes tree. It looked comfortable and warm, and he could imagine Emily in it. She was such a contradiction—sweetness and delicacy, yet strength and stubbornness. Then he thought again about holding her baby in his hands.

Switching off the light, he closed his eyes, feeling as if he'd dropped into somebody else's life.

The next morning, Slade let Mark sleep. The boy was going to miss school, but welcoming his mother and new sister home from the hospital was an important event. After Slade showered, he wrapped a towel around himself and went downstairs to dress, knowing when Emily was around, he'd have to make sure he had clean clothes upstairs.

After he tended to the animals, he started scrambled eggs and toasted Emily's bread in the oven. He'd just set the toast on the table when Mark came in. "You stayed upstairs last night," Mark said, looking pleased. "I had to get up for a drink of water and checked to make sure."

Glancing at the small boy curiously, he carried their plates to the table. "I told you I would."

Mark shrugged. "Dad used to tell me he'd do things, too, but he didn't."

Whether he should or not, Slade decided to pursue this subject a little. "What kind of things?"

"Playing ball, riding, goin' fishin'. He'd say he was gonna do it, but we never did."

When Slade took the chair around the corner from Mark, he offered, "Maybe he was too busy. Running a ranch is a lot of work."

"Mom's never too busy."

Slade suspected Emily always did what she said she was going to do. "I guess you miss your dad a lot."

Mark glanced at Slade and thought about it for a moment. "I guess."

Then Slade did the unforgivable by making a comment he hoped Mark would respond to. "I guess your mom does, too."

But Mark just shrugged again, lifted his piece of toast and bit into it.

That's what you get for trying to pump a child for information.

After breakfast Slade returned to Emily's room. Looking embarrassed the night before, she had asked him if he'd bring the denim jumper and white blouse hanging in her closet, as well as more personal items from one of her drawers, to the hospital the next morning. He had assured her it was no problem. But when he opened her closet, he couldn't help but finger the fabric of a navy-blue dress hanging there. He'd never stood in front of a woman's closet like this before. Granted, he'd had his affairs, always taking care, protecting himself as well as the woman. But he'd never stayed in their bed very long or they in his.

Quickly grabbing everything Emily had requested, he went downstairs, called to Mark and they climbed into the van.

Emily smiled at Slade when he arrived at her hospital room with Mark in tow. She looked bright and rested and absolutely beautiful. But he knew it would be a mistake to tell her that.

"I forgot about clothes for the baby," she said sheepishly. "So she'll have to come home in her hospital things."

"I don't think she'll mind," Slade teased her.

After Emily hugged and kissed Mark, she motioned to the jumper. "I'll be ready to leave as soon as I get dressed. The papers are all signed."

While Emily dressed, Slade and Mark waited at the front desk. The nurse finally wheeled her and the baby out. As they took the elevator down to the lobby, Emily looked up at him, and the glow on her face as she held her newborn wrapped itself around Slade's heart.

"It's a good thing I still have everything from

when Mark was born, or I wouldn't be ready for this."

"I'll have to come into town for gas. I can pick up anything you need."

Suddenly her smile slipped away. "You've done enough already, Slade. We're not your responsibility."

"Maybe not, but I couldn't let you have your baby alone in the van, could I?"

She didn't answer him and broke eye contact, looking down at the baby.

Everyone was quiet on the ride home.

Once they were back at the ranch, Slade helped Emily climb out of the van. As she walked slowly beside him cuddling Amanda, he kept a close watch. Once inside, she laid Amanda on the sofa while she took off her coat.

"You'd better rest for a while," Slade advised her. "Can you manage the steps?"

"I can. Just slowly."

"I'll come up with you and help you settle in."

Tears pricked in Emily's eyes. Slade was being so kind, and she didn't know what she'd do without him right now. That thought scared her almost as much as being close to him did.

At her bedroom doorway, she saw the made bed. "You didn't have to straighten up."

"Mark asked me to sleep up here last night. I just stayed on top of the covers."

Her cheeks pinkened. "I intended to turn the sewing room into a nursery. I've emptied it of everything but the machine, but didn't get around to bringing the crib from the attic. Do you think you could get it for me?"

"Sure can. Do you want it in there or in here? If I have extra time, I could make the room look more like a nursery if you want."

"I'd love to have pale pink walls..." she said, but she didn't finish. "Just put the crib in here for now. That'll be fine. The steps to the attic go up from the sewing room."

Emily laid Amanda in the middle of the bed. After Mark went up to the attic with Slade on the pretext of helping, she sat beside her baby, simply looking down at her, not quite believing this beautiful little girl was hers. Gently Emily brushed Amanda's downy brown hair across her forehead, remembering the look on Slade's face as her baby had come into the world.

Slade.

She hated depending on a stranger like this, but the doctor had told her she should rest today *and* tomorrow. The problem was—Slade was becoming more than a stranger...much too fast.

When he returned to her room with the folded crib, he set it down. "I wiped down the crib so you don't have to worry about it being clean. Mark found a box of old toys up there, and he's going through them to see if Amanda might like any of them." Slade's amused tone told her he hadn't tried to persuade her son differently.

"I guess I'll have to teach Mark how to be a good big brother."

"I don't think it will take much teaching." Slade opened up the crib, made sure it was sturdily set and then put the springs and mattress inside that were sitting beside the chest in Emily's room.

As Emily stood to get the sheets she'd washed

from her bottom chest drawer, Slade blocked her way. He was standing at the foot of the crib. "How are you feeling? And don't tell me you're fine."

Slade smelled like soap and man and she pictured him sleeping in her bed. "But I *am* fine. I have a beautiful baby girl who I didn't even know yesterday, and I'll have years to find out all about her."

Slade's blue gaze was gentle as he looked down at her. "You're a very special woman, Emily Lawrence."

She hadn't felt special in a very long time, nor pretty, nor even thought about attracting a man. But here she was standing in front of Slade Coleburn, embarrassed because he'd paid her a compliment, yet unable to take her eyes from his. What was it about this man?

When his hand came up, she knew he was going to touch her, and she knew she should step away.

Chapter Three

But Emily couldn't step away. Not with Slade's very blue eyes becoming more intense. Not with her heart racing, and definitely not when his roughened hand gently stroked her cheek. He seemed to move closer, but maybe she swayed toward him. She shut her eyes as if that could somehow block all of the feelings swirling inside of her. Yet when his lips brushed sensuously over hers in more of a tease than a kiss, she couldn't block anything. Feelings like this were a startling surprise. She hadn't known much satisfaction with Pete. After their marriage, he'd been concerned with getting his needs met. This brief touching of lips held more pleasure and more tender consideration than she'd ever felt with Pete.

How could that be? This man was a stranger. She'd only known him—

Amanda's small cries broke the silence.

Slade stepped away and when Emily opened her eyes, she saw questions in Slade's and had too many herself. Good Lord, what had happened to her? She'd just had a baby. A baby who needed her. She shouldn't be standing this close to a man who wandered from state to state, let alone be kissing him.

Flustered, her cheeks hot, she turned away from Slade and went to the bed to pick up her daughter. What had happened with him just now wouldn't happen again. Her hormones must be in an uproar. That was all.

And if Slade brought it up?

She'd tell him point-blank that she had two children to raise and had no room in her life for a wanderer.

Cuddling her daughter close, Emily glanced at Slade and said, "I have to feed her."

"Do you have bottles and everything you need?" he asked, his voice husky. "With her coming early—"

"I'm going to breast-feed."

It was a quiet declaration in the small bedroom, but the implications were more far-reaching than feeding her daughter. She saw a look come into Slade's eyes as if he were imagining it. After a moment she broke eye contact and crossed to the rocker, almost trembling at the idea of his watching her.

"Is there anything you need?" he asked in a low voice.

Breathing space popped into her mind, but she didn't say it, she just shook her head.

"I'll see if Mark is finished in the attic, then we'll try to put something together for lunch."

"Slade, I don't expect you to—"

"Help you?" he finished. "You need some help,

Emily, so you might as well get used to the idea. At least for a little while."

"But you have business in Billings."

"It's waited this long, it can wait a few more days."

Emily's cuddling had quieted her daughter for a few minutes, but now Amanda let out a high-pitched wail that said she was definitely tired of waiting. Slade simply gave Emily a slight deferential nod, then left the room, closing the door behind him.

Unbuttoning the top buttons of her jumper, and then her blouse, she bared her breast. As her daughter rooted for the nipple and then suckled, Emily was overwhelmed by the feelings of tenderness and love for her new baby. At the same time, she heard Slade's boot-falls on the steps. She remembered his kiss, then she blocked it from her mind.

Slade knew his way around a kitchen better than the average man. He'd had to fend for himself early and though he was most familiar with microwaves and hot plates, he knew how to use a stove. As he set Mark to cleaning up some of the toys he'd found in the attic, Slade warmed soup on the stove and sliced Emily's crusty bread. Just the thought of her upstairs feeding her baby...

He shouldn't be having these thoughts. She was a new mother. His stay here was only temporary, and he knew better than to get attached to her or to Mark. For years he'd known attachments spelled heartache.

Yet he couldn't help glancing at Mark fondly as he pulled a wooden stringed toy across the floor. "Why don't you go upstairs and ask your mom if she's about ready for lunch? Tell her I'll bring it up." No way was he going up to that room and taking the chance of finding her still feeding Amanda. There was enough tension between them already when they got within a foot of each other. Maybe it was just him. Maybe she didn't feel anything. Yet she hadn't backed away earlier.

"Can we go upstairs and eat with her?" Mark asked hopefully.

Not sure how much to say, Slade decided to keep it simple. "Having a baby is hard work and your mom's pretty tired. I think it would be a good idea today if we give her some time to herself so she can rest. If she's up to it, we can all have supper together tonight."

"Okay," Mark mumbled with a frown, but then looked animated again. "Can I go outside with you this afternoon?"

"If your mom says it's okay."

As Mark ran up the steps, Slade went to stir the soup and immediately dropped the hot spoon that he'd left in the pot on the stove. "Damnation." He'd better keep his mind on what he was doing. He'd better watch every step he took.

A short while later, while Mark buttered himself a slice of bread, Slade took a large plate with a bowl of soup, two slices of bread and a glass of milk up to Emily. He stopped outside the door when he heard her soft voice singing a lullaby. A curling feeling tightened his chest and he took a deep breath, then he rapped on the door.

"Come in," she said.

The sun had started its afternoon journey and beamed through the window between curtain panels, flickering on blond strands in Emily's hair. She looked lovely bathed in sunlight, holding her child, and he wondered again what kind of man her husband had been and if she still loved him.

"Are you hungry?" he asked.

"Not really, but I know I have to eat and eat well for Amanda's sake. We'll have to talk about supper. There are some things I can't have because of...well, feeding her."

"How about meat loaf?" he asked. "I saw ground meat down in the freezer."

"As long as you go easy on the seasoning," she said with a shy smile. "I wouldn't think most men would know how to make a meat loaf."

"I'm not most men." He set her lunch down on the dresser. "I know how to mash potatoes, too."

"Then you'll be Mark's friend for life. Mashed potatoes are his favorite."

A friend for life. He could hardly grasp the concept. "Mark says you don't mind if he follows me around this afternoon."

"I don't mind if you don't."

"I can keep him busy so you can rest. The thing is—if you need me for something..."

"I'll be fine, Slade. After I change Amanda, I'll eat and then rest for a while."

But Slade's mind was still on her being alone in the house. "If you do need me, just hang a pillowcase out the window. I'll make sure I look up here every now and then."

Fussing with the pink blanket wrapping Amanda, Emily looked down at her child. "You know, don't you, that you're earning more than your room and board. I'm never going to be able to repay you."

"There's no call for repaying generosity, Emily. It just goes along with telling the truth, and doing an honest day's work for an honest day's pay."

At that she looked at him pensively, and her gaze made him uncomfortable. "If you need anything else, just holler. If we don't answer back, just hang that pillowcase out."

Before he got lost in the soft brown of her eyes, he left the room and closed the door.

The afternoon passed quickly as Mark ran in Slade's wake, helping him do chores, groom the horses and attach weather stripping where it was needed. When they took a break and went inside in the late afternoon, Slade taught Mark the fine art of making meat loaf. The little boy was eager to learn and enjoyed squishing his just-washed fingers into the meat, egg and bread crumb mixture. While Mark was washing up, Slade went upstairs to check on Emily. He'd glanced often at the bedroom window but no pillowcase hung from its sill.

Her door was cracked a few inches and he pushed it open slowly. Lying on the bed curled on her side, her hands tucked under her cheek, she looked beautiful and peaceful and he had to remind himself that she was off-limits. She'd swaddled the baby in the pink blanket and Amanda was sleeping, too. Emily hadn't bothered with the afghan at the foot of the bed, and Slade crossed to it quietly, unfolded it, and gently covered her.

She opened her eyes.

"I didn't mean to wake you. I thought you might be a little cold."

"Thank you."

"Go back to sleep," he said, his voice gravelly.

Her eyes fluttered closed again and her breathing became even. Slade stood watching Emily and her baby, his gaze going from one to the other until he felt something he'd never felt before. He didn't understand what it was.

Emily came downstairs at suppertime with Amanda as if she couldn't bear to part from her. Slade guessed that mother and child were bonding. Before she sat down to eat, she looked up at him. "I have one more favor to ask."

He knew how hard it was for her to admit she needed help, so he didn't tease her, just waited.

"There's a cradle up in the attic. Could you bring it down here so I'll have a place to put Amanda?"

"Sure, no problem. I saw it when I was up earlier. It looks old."

"It was mine when I was a baby. My father made it for me."

The differences between him and Emily gripped Slade. She knew about family and roots and belonging. He knew nothing about any of those.

Emily complimented him on the meal more than once. She ate well and looked rested, and he'd bet she'd have her strength back in no time. That thought didn't settle well. He liked her depending on him. No one had ever depended on him before.

After supper, Emily let Mark hold Amanda and count each one of her toes. He seemed enthralled by the infant, afraid to touch her, afraid to get too close. A while later, Slade suggested he and Mark play a card game.

Emily sat on the sofa, crocheting a sweater for her daughter, every once in a while looking over at them with a pensive look. When Amanda began crying, Emily said, "I'm going to take her upstairs to feed her. Mark, you get into your pajamas. It'll soon be bedtime."

The problem was, when Mark's bedtime came and slowly slipped by, Amanda was still fussing. It was an hour past Mark's bedtime when Slade went upstairs and peeked into Emily's room. She was walking the fussy baby, rocking her and singing to her.

"Is something wrong?" Slade asked, worried because Amanda couldn't seem to get settled.

"I don't think so. Babies have fussy spells. Mark's was always from midnight to 2:00 a.m."

"I guess after having one baby, it's a little easier."

"I'm not as scared this time. With Mark I worried if I was doing everything right or everything wrong."

"I can put Mark to bed if you like." Amanda was crying again and it was obvious that Emily didn't want to leave her.

Emily raised her voice over the crying. "Tell him to come in here first, so I can say good-night. You don't have to read him a story—"

"I don't mind reading him a story, Emily."

Their gazes met, hers filled with gratitude, and he found himself wanting something other than thanks. He turned away to take care of Emily's son.

Mark said good-night to his mother, brushed his teeth, then said his prayers. But after he got into bed, he was frowning.

"What's wrong, partner? Think I can't read a story as good as your mom?" Slade asked.

"Mom *always* puts me to bed."

Thinking about Emily mothering Amanda and Mark on her own, Slade offered, "Things might change a little bit now. Babies need a lot of care."

"Why is she crying so much?"

Slade wasn't at all sure, but he figured he might as well try to give Mark an explanation he'd understand. "Amanda was safe and happy and comfortable growing in your mom's body for all these months. It was warm and dark and cozy in there, I guess. Now, she came into this big, old world and there's lights and noise and hot and cold and just lots of things she's got to get used to."

"How long does it take?" Mark asked, looking worried.

"Well, I'm not quite sure about that, but I imagine in a month or two, things will get easier."

Mark didn't comment on that. He just picked up the book he'd laid beside him and handed it to Slade.

After Slade put Mark to bed and turned off the boy's light, he could still hear Amanda crying behind Emily's closed door. He rapped on it, and at her muffled "Come in" opened it a few inches. "Is there anything I can do?"

She shook her head. "I was going to buy a pacifier but I didn't. She'll settle down eventually."

"I thought I'd run into town tomorrow, get that gas and anything else you need."

All of Emily's attention was on her daughter as she rocked her back and forth in her arms, then stood and walked around the room.

"If you need me, yell. I'll be in my room," he said.

When Emily just nodded, he felt as if he were

intruding, as if she didn't really want him there. But then again, maybe she didn't want any man in her life or helping her out. Stepping into the hall, he closed her door once again, then went downstairs.

It was almost midnight as Slade lay on his back on the bed, one arm crossed under his head while he stared into the dark. Amanda had stopped crying a short while ago. He'd heard the creaking of the floor above him as Emily rocked her baby. He could imagine her feeding her. He could imagine...

Turning onto his side, he threw his arm out over the quilt. But sleep eluded him. Images flitting through his mind wouldn't give him any peace. Concentrating on his trip to Billings the next day, he made a list in his head. He'd stop at the courthouse first and see if he could search through some public records. Maybe he'd get some answers. Maybe he'd find his twin brother.

Some of the tension was finally leaving his body when he heard the sound of running water in the kitchen. A spoon clattered into the sink, and he sat up. He should stay right here. He should just keep his eyes shut till he fell asleep. But the thought of Emily in the kitchen made him grab his jeans that he'd tossed over the straight chair beside his bed. He slid into them and pulled a flannel shirt from the closet, not bothering to button it, not bothering with shoes or socks.

Coming into the kitchen, he saw her pouring milk into a mug. Then she set it in the microwave to warm. When she turned to face him, he saw the surprise in her eyes. "I thought you'd be asleep," she murmured. "I didn't mean to disturb you."

"I wasn't sleeping."

Her hair softly waved along her cheek. She was wearing a pink flannel nightgown with a ruffle around the neck. Her robe was pale blue and fuzzy and looked as if it had seen a few winters. Her slippers were pink, too, and looked soft and comfortable. Everything about Emily made Slade want to take her in his arms, hug her and keep her safe.

Sure, safety is exactly what's on your mind, a voice in his head scolded.

To drown it out, he asked, "I guess Amanda settled down?"

"For the time being." Emily gave him a small smile, scooting her eyes away from the open shirt and his bare chest.

Crossing to the counter, Slade lifted muffins wrapped in tinfoil. Emily had asked him to take them out of the freezer earlier and they'd eaten them with supper. But a few of them had been left over.

"Interested?" He nodded toward the muffins.

"Sure," she replied as the microwave beeped. "But let's go into the living room. I'll be able to hear Amanda easier in there. Maybe when you go to town tomorrow, you can get me a baby monitor. I have an advertisement for one upstairs."

As they moved to the living room, he suggested, "Just jot things down, and I'll get whatever you need."

He could have taken the chair across from the sofa. Instead, he sat on the sofa cushion a few inches from Emily and opened the tinfoil.

When he offered her one of the muffins, she set her mug on the coffee table. "Thanks, Slade."

"You made them," he said with a grin.

"You know what I mean. Thank you for staying

and helping, for putting Mark to bed tonight. The list is growing. I don't know if I can ever repay you."

"I told you. No repayment is necessary." His voice was gruff as he avoided her eyes and broke a muffin in half.

There was silence for a minute or so as Emily broke off a piece of hers and popped it into her mouth. Slade couldn't help but glance at her. She had such a beautiful profile, such sweetly curved lips.

"You said you're going into Billings tomorrow. Will you be gone all day?"

"I'm not sure."

"Sorry. I didn't mean to pry."

"No. You weren't. It's just..." He drove his hand through his hair. "I'm not sure what I'll find."

Her gaze met his, and he couldn't tell what she was thinking. When she finally asked, "Are you looking for a woman?" he was surprised at the question and then felt some male satisfaction. Did she care if he was?

"No," he answered, not wanting to string her along. "I'm looking for my brother."

Was that relief he saw in her brown eyes?

"You don't know where he lives?"

He could evade the subject or he could dive straight into it with her. If he didn't give her information about his life, she certainly wouldn't give him information about hers, and he was getting more curious about what kind of marriage she'd had and what kind of man Pete Lawrence had been.

"I didn't grow up like most folks," he said.

When her gaze met his, he gave a shrug as if it

didn't matter. "Most kids have parents—at least one—and a home. But I never knew my parents. I was brought up in a boys' home."

"Slade, I'm sorry."

"Don't be. The people who took care of us kept us fed and clothed. Most of them were nice people. But it wasn't like having a real family. Kids came and went. So did the staff."

"Was your brother there with you?"

"I didn't know I had a brother, not until a couple of months ago. The home in Tucson where I grew up closed its doors. The whole system is different now and so are the kids. I was working on a ranch in Idaho when I got a letter from there." Every Christmas he sent the home a donation, and they must have kept track of his address. "With the letter I found a copy of my mother's death certificate and two birth certificates. One was mine, the other my brother, Hunter's. The birth dates are the same. The time of birth was five minutes apart."

"You have a twin?"

"Looks that way. There was a letter telling me Hunter had been adopted privately when we were eight months old. And there was a note on the certificates that copies had been forwarded to an address in Billings the same date as everything that was sent to me. I tried to contact authorities in Tucson for more information, but no one knew anything. All of it happened too long ago."

"Do you think your brother's in Billings?"

"I guess I can hope, but there isn't a phone number there for a Hunter Coleburn. I'm going to dig around public records, ask a few questions, go to the address. If I can't turn up anything, then I guess I'll hire a private investigator.''

"That will be expensive," Emily murmured.

"I know, but I have a nest egg tucked away."

"I wasn't trying to find out—"

"I know you weren't. But since I left Tucson when I was eighteen, I haven't had much call to spend money. A man doesn't need much when he's working or on the road."

"I guess you've never lived in one place very long."

"Nope. I went where I could find work, construction jobs, ranching. So I've pretty well traveled the South and Northwest. Have you ever been outside of Montana?"

She finished her muffin and put her napkin on the coffee table. "Never. I haven't been any farther than Helena. Dad took me there one time for a rodeo."

"What about your husband?"

"Pete grew up here like I did. And he didn't have any desire to...well, to see anyplace different."

There was something in the tone of her voice, something that made him want to pry a little more. Yet he didn't want her backing off. It was better if he asked questions one at a time, spaced apart.

Picking up her milk, she took a few sips and then set it back down. She looked nervous for a moment and then she asked, "How long do you think you'll be staying?"

"I don't know. It depends on what I find in Billings." Then he added, "It depends on how long you might need me here."

"You won't be adding to your nest egg if you stay here."

"I told you, I don't need much."

The way she was looking up at him, it was as if she was trying to figure him out. Her brown eyes were soft, her lips glistened from her sips of milk. The sleeve of her robe brushed against his shirt as he shifted slightly toward her. "You're a beautiful woman, Emily."

Her cheeks grew rosy and she shook her head. "I think you've been working around men and cows too long."

He laughed, and she smiled, and good sense couldn't keep him from slipping his hand under her silky hair. He waited to give her time to lean away, to give her time to think, to give her time to accept the idea of him kissing her.

So many thoughts ran through Emily's mind as Slade looked down at her. So many feelings thumped with each beat of her heart. What was she doing sitting here when she knew what would come next? She'd told herself she should stay away from him, but there was something about Slade that was so compelling, something about his blue eyes that made her want to just float right into them. And there was something about his strength and gentleness that called to a deep place inside of her. A kiss from Slade Coleburn...

He bent his head, and she lifted hers. She was trembling before his breath even whispered over her lips, and then he didn't do what she expected. Maybe she'd expected some hard, hungry demand. That's what she'd always gotten from Pete. But this was Slade, and already he'd shown her such gentleness.

First there was the soft nuzzle of his lips beside

hers and the feel of his cheek grazing hers. His scent was male and outdoors, and she couldn't believe the need that gripped her, to have his mouth cover hers. Instead he teased her, first with his lips, then with his tongue, and suddenly she was kissing him as she'd never kissed a man before. Her senses reeled as the sensations of his taste and his touch and his gentleness overwhelmed her. This was a real man. This was a man who knew how to please. This was a man—

This was a man who would be in and out of her life maybe as quickly as a strike of lightning. She pushed away from him, disgusted with herself that she didn't have her priorities straight. She had children to think of and a ranch to run, and no time for a man who didn't know the first meaning of the word roots.

Skittering a good six inches away from him, she cleared her throat and tried to compose herself. "That can't happen again. I don't know what got into me."

"Emily..." His voice was husky and deep and vibrated through her with the same resonance as his kiss.

Still flustered, the thoughts in her head came flying out. "I'm a new mother. I shouldn't even be thinking about...there's no way I can..."

"Do you think I'd want to take more than a kiss?"

"Yes...no...I don't know. I don't know *you*."

Slade's jaw set and his blue eyes lost their warmth. "You don't know me? After what we've been through together? Well, I'll tell you something about me. I'm a man of my word. And I give you my word that I won't kiss you again until or unless you ask me to.''

He stood then and as he did, his shirt placket spread farther apart and she could see how thick the dark hair was on his chest, how taut his stomach muscles were. The ripple of excitement that skipped down her spine confused her as much as Slade did.

Before she could come up with an adequate response to his declaration, he said in a clipped tone, "Good night, Emily. If you need me, just pound on the floor again." With that he strode through the kitchen and down the hall. She heard the sound of his door closing.

Picking up her cup of milk, she stared at it and felt tears prick in her eyes. She didn't want to need a man, especially not Slade Coleburn.

And hell would freeze over before she asked him to kiss her again.

Chapter Four

The tack slipped through Slade's fingers as he held the weather stripping against the door frame. Taking another from his pocket, he hammered the stripping in place. When he finished, he glanced at Emily as she slid a casserole into the oven. She'd skittered around the past two days, staying as far from him as she could get, and it was getting frustrating. Just as frustrating as the dead end he'd run into in Billings. He might never find his brother.

Hammering in another tack, he realized he was letting Emily distract him from his search. Maybe he shouldn't have gotten angry and said what he had the other night. Maybe he shouldn't have kissed her. But, dang it, she'd enjoyed that kiss as much as he had. "Enjoyed" didn't begin to cover it. It had thrown him for one very big loop. Emily might seem wholesome and ladylike and even quiet, but there was a deep passion inside of her that had lit his until he'd remembered she was a new mother, a recent widow and as she'd pulled away, a woman who didn't want him to kiss her again. At least that's what she'd said.

So be it.

From in the living room, the sound of Amanda's crying began low and increased in volume. Emily glanced at the kitchen clock and he knew what she was thinking. Mark would be home from school in about five minutes, and she was usually there to welcome him at the bus stop.

"Go ahead and feed her. I'll go get him," Slade said.

The volume of Amanda's crying stayed loud.

"I was hoping she would sleep so I could meet him today," Emily said with a sigh.

"Maybe on Monday. Don't worry about it." After a few moments, he added, "I'll tell him he can ride with me tomorrow to check the water troughs." Hammering in a final tack, Slade picked up the one that had fallen. After he laid the hammer and the remaining tacks on the table, he grabbed his hat from the rack and his coat from the hook. "Be back before you know it."

"Thanks, Slade."

He was getting tired of her thanks. He'd rather see her smile at him as if she meant it.

When Mark hopped down the step from the bus, he saw Slade and frowned. Hefting his backpack onto his shoulders, he asked, "Where's Mom? Is she feeding Amanda again?"

Slade thought making light of it might be the best way to handle it. "Your sister does seem to eat an awful lot, doesn't she?"

Mark gave him a sideways glance.

The boy had been quiet since Emily had come home from the hospital. Much too quiet. But Slade didn't know what to do about it, or if he should do anything. "How would you like to ride out with me tomorrow and check the cattle?"

"I bet Mom won't let me. She'll say it's too cold."

"I already asked her."

But even this didn't bring a smile from the little boy. He just looked sad as they walked the rest of the way up the road to the house.

Once inside, Mark looked around but didn't see his mom. "She's probably upstairs in her room again," he muttered.

Slade knew why she was and felt at fault where that was concerned. He and Emily were going to have to have a talk or there was going to be more than a little trouble with her son. Slade would bet his boots on it.

Not long after Mark came home, Emily returned downstairs with Amanda and laid her in the cradle in the living room. She tried to talk to her son about his day at school, but Mark's replies were one syllable and he didn't seem inclined to talk.

Emily looked concerned as she took greens from the refrigerator to make a salad. "Maybe I'll have some time tomorrow to make some cookies. Do you want to help?" she asked Mark.

"Slade said I could go out riding with him."

"Yes, I know, but maybe tomorrow afternoon we could do it."

Mark's expression brightened some. "Okay."

But still the seven-year-old didn't have much to say during supper. Emily insisted she didn't need any help cleaning up afterward, so Slade taught the boy what he knew about tying knots that he'd learned from an older man on one of the construction crews. Mark tried several different kinds as Slade ruffled the boy's hair and told him he'd be an expert before he knew it. This night, unlike the two previous evenings, Amanda was asleep when it was time to put Mark to bed, but Emily had no sooner read him a story and tucked him in when Amanda began crying.

Feeling keenly the demands of both of her children, Emily wished Mark good-night, then went to feed her daughter.

Until she had Amanda settled, a good hour had passed. On her way downstairs she wondered if Slade had turned in, but then she heard the TV.

"Are both of them asleep?" he asked.

Emily paused on her way to the kitchen. "I hope so. I just came down to get a glass of milk, then I'm going to join them."

"We ought to talk," he said, switching off the TV with the remote.

"What about?"

Slade pulled his legs in and sat up straighter. When he looked at her, she always felt as if he was asking her questions, but she didn't know any of the answers. His flannel shirt was open at the neck and the hairs there reminded her of the dark furring on the rest of his chest. If she closed her eyes and thought about it, she could still feel his kiss.

"A couple of things. The other night for one," he stated.

"There's nothing to talk about," she told herself as well as him.

"There is if you jump away from me every time I get anywhere close to you."

"That's your imagination."

"I have an imagination, and I also have twenty-twenty vision. It has nothing to do with my imagination."

She was too tired to have this discussion now. She felt as if she hadn't slept in a week. Just making meals and feeding Amanda and doing laundry seemed to exhaust her. "I'm just feeling a little…awkward. That's all. I'm not used to having a man around."

"You had a husband around, didn't you?"

"That's different. You're a stranger, Slade."

"Not quite."

They were both remembering the night in the van when he delivered her baby. They were both remembering a brush of lips on lips and then a kiss that had shaken her to her very core. She turned toward the staircase. "I'm going to bed."

But he was on his feet and catching her arm before she managed the first step.

Just then Amanda began crying again and Emily sighed. "Slade, I promise we'll talk tomorrow. All right?"

His blue gaze kept her immobilized for a few long seconds and then he nodded. "All right."

As he released her arm and she mounted the stairs, she knew it was a conversation she couldn't escape. She knew he would say his piece, even if she didn't want to hear it.

The following morning, Slade and Mark rode out, and along with caring for Amanda, Emily tackled a stack of chores. She had every intention of spending the afternoon with Mark, but after lunch, her neighbor, who had just heard about the baby's birth, called and asked if she could visit the next day after church. Mavis O'Neill was a talkative woman and before Emily knew it, another half hour had slipped by. She was taking ingredients from the pantry for a batch of oatmeal cookies, when Amanda began crying. Emily took her daughter to the bedroom to feed her, and Amanda decided her fussy time was now. The afternoon vanished and although Mark didn't say anything, he was silent throughout supper.

Emily said cheerfully, "We can make the cookies after supper."

Mark kept his eyes on his plate. "Slade's going to show me card tricks after supper."

"Oh, I see. Well, how about tomorrow afternoon?"

"I thought you said Mr. and Mrs. O'Neill were coming over."

Emily sighed. "Tomorrow evening, then."

"Whatever," Mark said with a shrug that told her better than words that he didn't think it would happen. Emily felt guilty and sad and not at all sure what to do next. About Mark or Slade.

When she put Mark to bed that night, her son wouldn't meet her gaze.

"Mark, before Amanda was born, we talked about you having a baby sister. I know it seems as if I have to take care of her a lot, but I promise you we'll spend some time together tomorrow."

"Don't worry about it. I got Slade."

That idea *did* worry her. "Honey, I don't know how long Slade's going to stay. He's only passing through."

Mark's expression told her he didn't like that idea at all. "He'll stay if we ask him to."

"He has concerns in Billings that have nothing to do with us. He's searching for a brother he never knew, and that search could take him far away from here."

Mark still avoided her eyes as he slid into bed and pulled the covers up to his chin. "Good night, Mom."

"Mark, you know if there's anything you want to talk about..."

He shook his head.

Emily knew from past experience with her son that he'd open up on his terms...when he was ready. It was obvious he didn't want to talk about any of it now. She'd just have to try again tomorrow.

Leaning close she gave him a long hug, said, "I love you," then released him.

But Mark didn't reply.

Tenderly she brushed his wavy hair across his forehead. At the doorway she stopped. "Good night."

After he mumbled "G'night," he turned on his side away from her, and she closed his door.

By the time Emily took a quick shower, it was time to feed her daughter. She was sitting in the rocker, humming to Amanda but thinking about Mark when there was a sharp rap on the door. She didn't have time to cover herself before it opened.

"Emily, we've got to talk. Mark just came downstairs and asked me—" The thrust of Slade's words stopped abruptly as he stared at her with her daughter at her breast.

Their gazes locked, and Emily saw something so

powerful in Slade's eyes it scared her. It was a mixture of longing and desire and something entirely foreign to her. She quickly looked around to see if there was anything she could cover herself with, but found nothing.

Seeing her discomfort, Slade crossed to the crib, lifted a blanket and handed it to her. She hastily threw it to her shoulder, covering her breast and the baby.

"All right. It's finally happened," he said. "I saw you. Emily, women have been feeding their children in public since the dawn of time. Why do you have to come up here and hide every time you do it?"

She didn't understand the frustration and anger behind his tone. "You've no right to tell me how to take care of my daughter."

"You may be taking care of your daughter, but you're not taking care of your son. He just came downstairs and asked me how long I was staying. When I told him again I don't know, he ran back up here and now he won't talk to me."

Emily knew Mark was hurting. And it looked as if this time maybe she shouldn't wait for him to talk. Rather, she'd have to force the issue. Getting back on her feet, caring for a newborn, wanting to make time for her son but not knowing how, seeing the sparks of desire in Slade's eyes and fearing her growing feelings for him, all made tears well up. She tried to blink them away, but one rolled down her cheek.

When she swiped at it, Slade's expression softened and he crouched down in front of her. "Oh, Emily, I didn't mean to make you feel bad. After you're finished here, we'll talk. All right?"

She nodded, realizing she had to face her desire for Slade as well as whatever was bothering Mark.

Tears continued to fill her eyes even after Slade left the room, and as her daughter suckled at her breast, Emily brushed them away, knowing she wasn't a crying type of woman, wishing her hormones would settle down to normal.

After she gently laid Amanda in her crib, she blew her nose, splashed water on her eyes and ran a brush through her hair. She looked a fright. Checking on Mark, she saw that he was asleep. As she watched the rise and fall of his breaths, she knew he wasn't pretending. Leaving his door open slightly, she went downstairs.

Slade motioned to a mug of milk on the coffee table. "I thought you might want that."

His kindness almost made tears fill her eyes again. She blinked quickly and composed herself, then sat on the sofa beside Slade, yet a good six inches away from him. "I know I need to spend more time with Mark. I just didn't realize how difficult handling two children would be. I was happy when I found out I was pregnant, even though Pete was gone. Another child to love seemed like a blessing. I really never thought about one taking time from the other."

Slade shifted toward her. "I'm sorry if I was...abrupt with you upstairs, but you have to stop running off and hiding with Amanda. That's part of the problem. Mark sees you giving all this time and attention to her and he figures he doesn't count."

"But he can come in," she said defensively, not ever meaning to shut her son out.

"Emily, you have the door closed to keep me out, and I understand that. Sort of. What do you think is going to happen if I see you breast-feeding your daughter?''

The problem was that she didn't know what she wanted to happen. "It's a matter of privacy, Slade."

"No. It's a matter of me being a man and you being a woman and having a couple of kisses between us. If I were a woman, we wouldn't even be having this discussion. You'd be feeding Amanda in the living room or the kitchen or wherever it was convenient."

"If you were a woman, I wouldn't—"

"Wouldn't what?" he asked gently.

She wouldn't hold her breath each time he came into the room. She wouldn't tremble when he got really close. She wouldn't feel something inside her stir when his eyes met hers. "Well, you're not a woman, Slade, and it's not like you're a member of the family."

Her statement made his jaw set, and the nerve on it work. "Do you ever intend to take Amanda out of this house?"

"Of course I do."

"So what are you going to do then if you have to feed her?"

Somehow with Mark she'd always managed to find a private spot. "It's not hard to get away from other people."

"Maybe not, but I think you're going to have to find a way to include your son in this or you're going to have big trouble."

Slade's words rang true. If Mark started pulling away from her now, what would happen when he was older? "I suppose during the day I could feed her down here and stay covered. I just don't want to feel as if you're…''

"Wanting to take a look?" he asked practically.

"Yes."

"This is your house, Emily. These are your children. I'll abide by whatever rules you set up."

"It's not that simple," she said softly and then looked away. Part of her *wanted* Slade to watch, and that shocked her. "Look, I appreciate what you're saying and I'll work something out."

"Why is it so hard for you to accept help?" he asked, searching her face.

Her reply was quick in coming. "Because I don't want to ask anyone to do what's my responsibility. Asking for help makes me feel weak," she said in a burst, frustrated because he'd pressed her to put it into words.

He faced her more squarely. "You're the strongest woman I've ever met, but everybody has limits and I'd say both you and Mark have reached them."

In some ways, he was right. "What do you think I should do?"

"Let up a little. I can make a meal now and then. We can open a can of soup instead of you making it."

"That's more expensive," she said simply.

"I'll buy you soup for the next two weeks," he teased.

"That's exactly what I *don't* want." She'd had to fight with him to take money for the baby monitor he'd bought for her.

They stared at each other, neither of them blinking until finally Slade blew out a breath and muttered, "The most stubborn woman I've ever met."

She couldn't help but smile then. "At least I still take the blue ribbon for that."

Something changed in his eyes. They became deeper blue...mesmerizing. When he leaned toward her, she wasn't sure what he meant to do, but he reached out to her and let his thumb gently rest on her cheekbone.

She looked up at him, confused by a multitude of feelings, wanting his kiss yet wishing she could escape this pull toward him.

When he leaned away slightly, his voice was a husky temptation as he reminded her, "Remember what I said, Emily. Next time you have to ask."

Immediately she remembered the last kiss and her reaction to it. She'd thought it would be easy to stay away from him. She'd thought it would be easy *not* to ask. Pride made her draw herself up straight. "I'm going to have a talk with Mark tomorrow and maybe I can make some changes."

"Showing him would be better than telling him," Slade advised her with a knowing look that saw way too much.

"I'll keep that in mind," she said as she stood and turned toward the stairs.

"Emily, you forgot something."

She faced him again, wondering if he would take her in his arms....

But instead, he held out the mug of milk. "You might sleep better if you drink it."

She might sleep better if she could put Slade Coleburn out of her head. When she took the mug, their fingers brushed. He didn't move and neither did she. Telling herself she was too tired to play games, she murmured, "Good night," broke eye contact and started up the stairs.

"Sweet dreams, Emily."

There was no reason to glance over her shoulder because she knew if she did, she'd see the twinkle in Slade's eyes that would tell her he knew she might dream of him.

The following morning, Slade went outside to feed the animals and do some chores. Emily had been up and bustling around the kitchen with a new energy that Slade suspected came more from determination than from a good night's sleep. She acted as if she'd thought over a few things and made some decisions, but he had no clue as to what they were. She still avoided getting too close, and he remembered her looking up at him on the sofa last night. It had been damn stupid of him to set up the terms of the next kiss as stubborn as this woman was. He might never kiss her again. Disappointment at that thought sliced deep, but he shook it off and went about feeding the horses.

When he returned to the house, Emily was setting breakfast on the table—scrambled eggs, home fries, thick slices of toast. She called Mark and when he came down in his pajamas rubbing his eyes, she wore a cheerful smile and engaged him in conversation, or at least tried to. By the time he'd eaten most of his eggs, he was telling her about the turkey he'd made in art class on Friday.

"Thanksgiving is only a few days away," Emily said. "I guess I should see about getting a turkey."

"Are you sure you want to go to all that trouble?" Slade asked.

After a glance at Mark, she nodded. "It's Thanks-giving, Slade."

Thanksgiving had never meant very much to him, like most of the holidays. It was just another day when he knew he didn't belong to somebody. Since he hadn't met with any success looking for infor-mation about his brother in public records, he de-cided to take out ads in a few of the big papers from Chicago to Los Angeles. He was afraid to set his expectations too high, but he wanted to try this him-self before he hired a P.I.

"Why don't you make a list?" he suggested to her. "Mark and I can go in town and get everything we need. But we're only going to let you make the turkey if you promise to let us help. Right, Mark?" he nudged the boy in the arm.

Mark looked a bit surprised. "Sure. I can pull the bread apart for the stuffing."

Emily smiled at her son and took another sip of orange juice. Suddenly Amanda's cry came from the living room.

Mark's face fell.

But instead of rushing in to pick up her daughter, Emily said to her son, "Why don't you show me the turkey you made and get me your school papers from last week? I can look at them while I'm feed-ing Amanda."

Mark looked puzzled. "Really?"

Standing, Emily came around his chair to give him a hug. "Really. Bring them into the living room."

Slade's gaze met hers over her son's head. Ap-parently she had decided to make some changes and only good could come of it. Wanting to give her whatever space she needed, Slade stood, too. "Go on. I'll clean up in here. Then I'll be working in the barn."

When she smiled at him, Slade's heart felt like it turned over in his chest. It was a smile that made him believe they'd established some kind of understanding, as if she actually liked having him here. Before he left the house, he heard her talking to Mark about what he could expect from Amanda in the months to come—when she might smile and get her first tooth and then crawl.

He smiled when he heard Mark ask, "She won't be able to eat real food till then?" Chuckling, glad Mark and Emily were connecting again, Slade went to the barn.

About an hour later, Slade heard the flashy, new crew-cab truck before he saw it. It's silver finish gleamed in the sunlight. He'd heard Emily's phone conversation with her neighbor, Mavis O'Neill, and supposed she'd arrived. Intending to finish chores in the barn, he suddenly changed his mind when he spotted the driver of the truck. He was tall, wore a tan Stetson and a suede jacket with fringes. When he walked behind the older couple up to the house, Slade figured he must be a son or something. His interest piqued, Slade finished laying fresh straw in the stalls and went up to the house.

Going inside, he found everyone but Mark in the living room. The older lady with short brown curls streaked with gray was holding Amanda. Her husband, his grin softening burly features, was sitting beside her, looking on the baby fondly. But it was the younger man that drew Slade's attention. He had brown hair, green eyes and was standing much too close to Emily, gazing down at her as if she was the prettiest woman on earth. After Slade thought about it a minute, he supposed she was. She was wearing a black skirt that buttoned down the front and a red sweater that looked fuzzy to the touch. Whoever the man was, his arm was brushing hers and she looked as if she didn't care. Whenever *he* got that close...

Stepping into the living room, he cleared his throat loudly, keeping his gaze on Emily.

Her eyes met his and for a moment she looked uncertain. But then the man beside her was looking at Slade, too, and so was the older couple.

Emily's cheeks became rosy. "Slade, this is Mavis and Rod O'Neill and their son, Dallas. Everyone, Slade Coleburn. He's...ah, I've hired him on to help out."

Dallas frowned. "Mom should have told you I was coming home for Thanksgiving. I could have done anything that needed attention around here."

"You have your own concerns now with computerizing your dad's records and managing the herd," Emily said.

Denying the prickling jealousy he felt and wanting to keep things on an even keel, Slade extended his hand to the man. "It's good to meet you."

"Same here. Where are you from?" Dallas asked.

"I last worked on a ranch in Idaho, if that's what you're asking." Dallas's green eyes were intense, and Slade knew exactly what was on Dallas O'Neill's mind. "Emily checked out my references."

Emily moved between the men then and laid her hand lightly on Dallas's arm. "How about some coffee? Mavis and Rod?"

Mark practically flew into the room then, waving what looked like a paper plate with colored spokes pasted all around it. "See my turkey, Dallas?"

Dallas laughed and crouched down to the boy. "That looks like a fine turkey to me."

While Emily brewed coffee, small talk was strained until they got onto the subject of ranching. Slade learned that Dallas was earning a master's degree in animal science at the University of Illinois. He'd be finished at the end of summer, then he'd be home to stay. Besides building up his family's herd with what he'd learned, he trained horses, too.

As Emily listened to the hum of voices in the living room, she poured milk into a creamer, then took the bowl of sugar from the cupboard.

Mavis came into the kitchen and said, "Amanda fell asleep. I put her in her cradle. She's absolutely adorable."

"I think so, too," Emily said with a smile. She liked Mavis O'Neill and respected her. Her father and Rod O'Neill had been best friends all their lives, and their friendship carried over to her and Dallas. They'd gone through school together.

Lifting mugs from the wooden tree at the corner of the counter, Mavis glanced over at her. "How long has Mr. Coleburn been here?"

Emily had figured there'd be questions. Soon enough, neighbors other than Mavis and Rod would know Slade was staying here. Word got around. "He's been here about a week. He got stranded here last Sunday night when it snowed, and he slept out in the barn. And then, well, he's the one who delivered Amanda. I owe a lot to him."

Mavis's brow creased. "I see. How long is he staying?"

"He doesn't know yet and neither do I. He's looking for a relative." She didn't feel it was her place to tell Slade's story.

"You know there's going to be talk, don't you? Pete's been dead less than a year."

She and Mavis had never stood on ceremony. "I don't pay attention to talk. I didn't when Pete was alive, and I don't now that he's gone. Slade's a good man. I don't know what I would have done without him this past week."

"You can call me anytime—"

"Mavis, we've been through this. I don't like to impose. I'm giving Slade room and board in exchange for the chores he does."

"So he's staying in the house?" Disapproval was evident in her tone.

"He sleeps down here in Dad's old room. Everything's proper, Mavis." A little devil inside her head reminded her, *Except for that last kiss.* Emily quieted it by taking a package of muffins from the bread box.

"I don't plan on gossiping about this, but you know others will." Opening one of the cupboards, Mavis took out a plate and handed it to Emily. "I know, too, you have a mind of your own and you'll do what's right for you."

After she and Mavis carried the muffins and coffee into the living room, Emily sensed tension between the men.

Slade spoke first. "Dallas mentioned he mended some of your fence that was down. I told him I can handle that kind of thing. As long as I'm here."

Emily felt the war of wills between the two men and knew she had to settle it. First, she addressed Dallas's father. "I appreciate everything you've done for me while I was pregnant, Rod."

"And we've enjoyed your breads and cakes and pies," he said with a smile at his wife.

Crossing to Dallas with a mug of coffee, Emily handed it to him. "I appreciate your helping, too. But I'll be fine. And when Slade leaves, if I need you, I'll let you know."

"Promise?" Dallas asked with a twinkle in his green eyes that Emily knew came from the friendship they'd shared over the years.

"I promise," she returned.

There was silence in the room for a few moments until Slade stood. "It was good meeting you all, but I have chores in the barn."

His smile was strained and Emily knew he probably felt out of place, but she realized there was no point coaxing him to stay if he wanted to go. "You didn't drink your coffee. I'll put some in a thermos for you."

When Slade followed her to the kitchen, she felt his gaze on her. Pouring coffee into the same thermos she'd used the night he'd arrived, she finally glanced at him. "Is something wrong?"

"Nothing's wrong. I just have a question." His voice went deep and low. "What does Dallas O'Neill mean to you and how long has it been going on?"

Chapter Five

Slade's question shocked Emily. It not only insulted her, but it made her plain mad. "What do you mean, how long has it been going on? What are you accusing me of?"

His voice stayed low. "You never talk about your husband. You don't even have a picture of him around. And you seem right familiar with Dallas O'Neill."

"Familiar?" Her tone dropped as low as his as she glanced into the living room. "Dallas and I have known each other since we were kids. As far as my husband is concerned...that's none of your business. Neither is Dallas." She shoved the thermos at Slade.

But he wasn't giving up. "Were you and Dallas sweethearts?"

After letting out an impatient breath, she stated, "Dallas and I were and *are* friends. Always have been, probably always will be. Now I have to get back to my guests."

When she would have turned away from Slade, he snagged her arm. "Was your marriage unhappy?"

She didn't want to talk about it with him, not here, not now, maybe not ever. She felt guilty about the way Slade made her feel. She'd never experienced the tingling excitement and awareness with her husband that she felt with Slade. "Keep pushing, Slade, and I might decide I can do just fine without you here." Ignoring his intense stare, she went into the living room.

Emily didn't see Slade again until suppertime. When he came into the kitchen, he said, "I'm going to get a shower." His blue eyes were cold, and his smile was strained when he glanced at Mark.

"Mom helped me make a notebook of animal pictures for school. Want to see?"

"How about after supper?" He only waited for Mark's nod before he moved down the hall without looking at her.

A score of feelings tumbled around inside of Emily. The whole time she'd visited with the O'Neills she couldn't keep her mind off of Slade. Throughout supper the silence between them was obvious. What had her most upset was Slade's accusation that she had been unfaithful. He hadn't said it in so many words, but that's what he'd meant. How could he think that of her?

Something out of the ordinary happened after Slade helped Emily clean up the dishes. He retired to his room. He said he had some reading to do. She felt as if he were punishing her for wanting to keep her life private. Telling herself what Slade Coleburn did was none of her concern, she and Mark made cookies, then watched a family movie on TV.

She was feeding Amanda when Mark asked her, "Can I say good-night to Slade?"

"Maybe you'd better not bother him tonight. I'll tuck you in as soon as I'm finished feeding your sister."

Emily was grateful when Amanda fell asleep in her arms and didn't fuss after Emily laid her in her crib. Taking her time with her son tonight, she read him a story, listened to his prayers, kissed him and tucked him in.

But Mark looked up at her, puzzled. "Are you mad at Slade?"

She'd never lied to him, and she wouldn't start now. "I was earlier. He said some things I didn't like. But we'll work it out. Don't you worry."

"I don't want him to leave yet, Mom."

"I know you don't." And simply for her son's sake, she said, "I'll try to convince him to stay until after Thanksgiving anyway."

Though Mark looked far from satisfied, he nodded and she brushed his dark brown hair across his forehead tenderly, telling him good-night.

When she went downstairs, there was no sign of Slade. She could try to forget about what had happened between them today and go to bed, but she knew she wouldn't sleep. Her father had always told her, *You'll never get insomnia if you make peace with your day.* Unfortunately making peace with her day had to do with making peace with Slade.

But she'd never turned away from a chore simply because it was hard to do. With determination lifting her chin, she hurried down the hall and rapped softly on Slade's door.

After a few moments, he opened it. Still dressed in the green plaid flannel shirt and jeans he'd changed into after his shower, he looked handsome and virile and thoroughly masculine. Her mouth went dry. But then she realized his lips were almost clamped together and his jaw was set as if daring her to speak to him.

She took the dare. "We should talk."

"Seems to me that's what I wanted to do earlier and you didn't."

"Slade, I didn't knock on your door to argue with you."

After studying her carefully, he stepped closer. "Why did you knock? Sometimes talking takes a bit of arguing. Sometimes talking isn't very comfortable."

"All right," she said with resignation. "I knocked because I want to know what I ever said or did to make you think I could be unfaithful to my husband."

"Were you?" he asked simply.

All of her good, peaceful intentions exploded into a loud, "No." Before she could prevent it, tears came to her eyes and she turned away from him and headed down the hall. Maybe she was wrong about making peace with Slade. Maybe she was wrong about asking him to stay through the holidays even for Mark's sake.

In a few strides he caught up to her, hooked his hand over her arm and tugged her back to his room.

"I'm not going in there with you," she declared, pulling away from him. "That would prove what you think of me.'' In spite of her trying to will them away, tears rolled down her cheeks.

''Emily, I'm afraid you have no idea what I think of you.''

There was something in Slade's eyes that made her breath catch. She wasn't sure if he moved or if she did, but suddenly they were standing even closer than before.

His shirt almost brushed against her sweater as he said, ''I don't know much about marriages, but I know they can go bad. And I think Dallas wants to be more than friends with you,'' Slade concluded.

''He's been away, Slade. The last two years or so, we've only seen each other around the holidays.''

''Sometimes that's all it takes…when a man finds what he wants.''

''Dallas doesn't want me. And I don't want him. Not that way.''

Slade's gaze searched her face slowly, from her eyes to her nose, to her mouth, and back up again. ''I was jealous, and you're going to tell me I have no right to be. But you didn't skitter away from him like you do me.''

''I don't skitter away from you,'' she murmured.

He arched his brows. ''What would you call it?''

This close to him, with her heart thumping erratically and her breath coming faster, she knew she should run rather than skitter. ''I'm comfortable when I'm around Dallas. When I'm around you…''

''Yes?'' he prompted.

''I feel things I shouldn't. I just had a baby. I'm a widow. I—''

He slid his hand under her hair. ''You're a

woman, Emily. And I'm a man. I was attracted to you the first moment I laid eyes on you, and I told myself I shouldn't be."

"But I was pregnant."

"Yeah, I know, and now you're not, and nothing's changed except…I don't want what I'm feeling to be one-sided. Is it?"

Slade was the most honest man she'd ever met. "No," she confessed in a whisper.

After her admission, he didn't bend his head to kiss her, and he didn't put his arm around her. He just stood there with his hand under her hair, and she remembered what he'd said. He wouldn't kiss her again until she asked him to. But if she asked him to kiss her, she was afraid of the complications and the consequences. Not only to her, but to Mark. For all their sakes, she backed away from Slade until his hand was by his side.

"Do you want me to leave, Emily?" he asked, giving her a considering look.

"No. I told Mark I'd ask you to stay until after Thanksgiving. I know he'd like it if you'd stay through Christmas."

"What about you?"

"I'd like you to stay."

Slade was silent for a few moments. "All right. I'll stay through Christmas. And maybe we'll both get used to being around each other."

To her relief, he took a few steps toward his room. Before going in, he said, "I'll see you in the morning."

When he closed his door, Emily breathed a sigh of relief, knowing she'd never get used to Slade Coleburn being in her house, let alone in her life.

* * *

After Thanksgiving dinner, Slade leaned back in his chair and smiled at Emily. "Now that was a meal fit for a king."

"Even though you helped prepare it?" she asked teasingly.

"That made it even better. Right, Mark?" Mark had helped to mix up the dressing and stuff the bird, while Emily had concentrated on making cranberry-orange relish.

Mark nodded. "And the best part is Amanda slept through the whole thing." But after he said it he glanced at his mother uncertainly.

Ruffling her son's hair, Emily smiled. "Next year we'll be feeding her mashed potatoes and trying to keep her out of harm's way. You might wish she was a baby again once she's walking."

Slade could imagine Amanda, her hair longer, her eyes shining like her mom's as she toddled around the house.

"Speaking of helping." Emily looked directly at her son. "I have to make pies tomorrow for Saturday's bake sale. Are you going to lend me a hand?"

"I guess. Are we going to the bazaar?"

"What bazaar?" Slade asked.

"On the Saturday after Thanksgiving every year, our church sponsors a Christmas Bazaar. They have a bake sale, and ranchers' wives sell things they craft by hand. I usually make about ten pies."

"Ten pies? You've got to be kidding."

"No. It's a tradition, Slade."

"Don't you think that's a little ambitious?"

She shrugged. "I'll get started and then see how far I get. I have the supplies. It depends on how well Amanda cooperates."

"I'm sure everyone would understand if you skipped this year." He didn't want to see her tiring herself out and doing more than she should be.

But Emily's determined chin rose a notch. "I told Mavis I would bake pies, and I'm going to bake pies."

"All right, then I guess I'll have to help with the rolling pin." His blue eyes were steady on hers.

"Not if you have other things to do." Her tone was firm. It was a battle of wills again, and Slade knew he'd better drop the subject for the time being.

They were careful not to touch when they moved around the kitchen, scraping plates, putting away leftovers. It was as if they both knew they were walking a line they shouldn't cross.

Slade put the milk in the refrigerator, feeling as if he had to say something. "I've never celebrated holidays much."

Emily had started washing the dishes. She glanced at him, and their gazes held for a moment.

"I love holidays," she murmured. "Especially Christmas. The world just seems a softer place then. People are more giving, less selfish. I can't donate much to our church, but I can bake pies for the sale. They use the proceeds to help members of the congregation who need it."

Emily's life was so foreign to Slade—the way she was connected to everybody and everything. "I don't know much about traditions," he said quietly.

"If you stay through Christmas, Mark and I'll show you a few." Her expression was teasing but mostly sincere. Yet she used the word "if." It was as if she expected him to pack up his belongings and leave any day.

"I'll be here through Christmas," he told her again.

Later, at the kitchen table with a notepad, his checkbook and the addresses of major newspapers from Chicago to Los Angeles, Slade stamped one envelope after another, trying not to get his hopes up. There was a slim chance the ads would produce his brother, but only a slim chance. When he'd gone into Billings to the house where the birth and death certificates had been sent, a middle-aged woman had opened the door. He'd inquired about the previous owners, but she couldn't give him any information, just that she thought they'd moved to Colorado. Concentrating on sending more ads to Colorado newspapers than anywhere else, he sealed the last envelope and placed it on the pile.

Emily was sitting in the living room with Mark, and Slade could hear Amanda fussing. When he looked up at the clock above the kitchen sink, he saw it was past Mark's bedtime. The boy had seemed more settled again, happier, since Emily had made sure she was giving him more attention. Still, not being the only child had to be hard.

As Slade went into the living room, he could see Mark was trying to watch a football game above all the ruckus. Going over to Emily, he offered, "Why don't you let me take her while you put Mark to bed?"

Emily looked up at him, her eyes wide with surprise. "You've never even held her before."

"That's true, but I don't imagine there's a whole lot to it. It can't be any worse than holding onto a squirming piglet."

Emily's laugh floated free into the room. "I guess not, but it could be noisier."

He shrugged. "Then again, maybe she'll settle down for me. Come on, hand her over."

Emily's expression was skeptical and more than a little worried.

"I'll be careful," he assured her. "I've watched you showing Mark how to hold her. I know I have to keep her head supported."

"He can do it, Mom. Slade's good at everything."

Slade chuckled. "I don't know about that."

Amanda was fussing again, halfhearted crying that Slade supposed was from her wanting to make her presence known, or wanting to keep her mom's attention. He held out his arms and Emily carefully placed Amanda in the crook of his elbow.

Taking the baby, blanket and all, he gazed down at her and tickled her under the chin. "Okay, little lady, we're just going to walk and talk and rock until your mom comes back. I promise I won't drop you."

Emily shook her head and rolled her eyes, as Amanda looked up at Slade and was suddenly very quiet.

"She must like your voice," Emily said softly.

"Then I'll just keep talkin'."

After Emily and Mark went upstairs, Slade walked Amanda around the room, talking to her as if she were Mark's age. He couldn't understand why folks cooed and mumbled funny things to babies as if they came from another planet. Finally he ended up at the window, pointing to the moon and showing Amanda how the stars formed pictures in the sky.

He was so involved in telling the baby about the Big Dipper and the sportsman with the bright star in his belt, that he wasn't aware of Emily coming downstairs again until she was practically standing at his elbow.

"So you're an expert on the night sky," she said with a smile.

"Not an expert. When I was a kid I got hold of a book about stars, the moon and the sun. At the home, nothing really belonged to any of us. I mean we didn't have toys or books of our own usually. But one of my teachers gave me that book because she said she thought I had potential. I wasn't exactly sure what that meant, but it seemed important, so I kept the book under my pillow and each night when everybody else was sleeping, I took it out and looked at it along with the sky."

Together he and Emily stared up at the moon through the frosted window.

Finally she said, "I'll take Amanda upstairs now."

"Do you want some warm milk before you turn in?"

"Sure. And help yourself to another piece of pie."

When Emily returned to the living room, an empty dish with only a few crumbs sat on the coffee table beside a mug of coffee. Her warm milk was just a few inches away from it. But Slade was standing at the window again, looking out, totally engrossed as if he saw more than the dark landscape. Only one dim light glowed near the stairs, but Slade's profile was distinct in the shadows, and she couldn't even guess at what he was thinking. He didn't move a muscle as she came toward him and she wondered if he'd heard her.

But then he said, "Today was special to me, Emily. More than you could ever know."

"It was special for us, too," she admitted, realizing it was so.

He faced her then with an intense look that should have scared her, but it didn't. It filled her with excitement instead.

"Am I still a stranger to you?" he asked. "Do you want me to keep my distance?"

She knew keeping her distance was safer. She knew labeling Slade a stranger was less complicated. But she couldn't lie to herself or to him. "You're not a stranger anymore. But I'm not sure what I want. My life's changed so in the past year."

"I think you do know what you want. At least for right now. And right now is all we ever have, Emily."

She'd lived day-to-day with Pete because she couldn't expect more. "Don't you have dreams?" she asked.

Without hesitating, Slade shook his head. "What's the point of thinking about something that might never be? I'd rather take what I have in hand and enjoy it as much as I can."

They were standing so close, surrounded by a night intimacy that reached from the dark sky into where they stood. The silence was almost loud, broken only by a creak of the house as cold wrapped around it.

"What do you want, Emily?" Slade prodded.

His male essence called to her and she knew exactly what she wanted at this moment, but she didn't know if she dared have it. She didn't know if she had the courage to ask for it, because that's what Slade expected her to do. That's what he'd told her she must do if she wanted to feel his lips again.

"I..." She stopped.

"What?" he asked again in a deep husky murmur that she guessed was supposed to be reassuring.

"Will you..." Her voice caught.

"Will I what?" he urged.

"Will you...kiss me?" The last two words came out in an embarrassed rush but that apparently didn't matter to Slade. His arms enfolded her and as he pressed her against him, he looked down at her, searching her face.

"What's wrong?" she whispered, thinking hell certainly must have frozen over because she'd never done anything so bold in her entire life.

"I never thought you'd ask."

Then with a slow bend of his head, his hot, firm lips touched hers. His tongue traced her upper lip, and she felt her legs go weak. He was holding her, but she wrapped her arms around his neck to make sure she didn't fall. Yet when she felt the hair at his nape, breathed in his scent, and gave herself up to the sheer pleasure, she felt as if she was falling into a deep whirlpool and would never come out again. His tongue was sensually wet, sensually rough, and so teasing. He left no surface of her lips untouched, untasted, uncoaxed. And when he slipped it between her lips, she thought she'd die from the sheer longing of wanting him there.

She didn't know herself as she hung on and expectantly waited for whatever he did next. Slade's expertise was obvious as he touched the tip of her tongue with his, teased her a little, then stroked her. She couldn't feel the floor under her feet and she realized he'd lifted her to his level so he could angle his mouth and kiss deeper. Everything swirled away except for the moment and Slade and the way he was making her feel. It wasn't only the pleasure... During her marriage, she'd lost the deep yearning for mating. Now she felt it with Slade. He made her feel beautiful, womanly, desired. Yet they couldn't do anything else for weeks and—

Anything else? What was she thinking of? She had to set an example for her children. She had to stick to the values she'd always believed in. Besides, in a few weeks, Slade could be gone. He'd as much as said he didn't believe in dreams or the future.

With that thought pounding in her head, her hand slipped to his shoulders and she pushed away. He was still holding her up, gazing at her, the silver desire in his eyes, almost as seductive as his kiss. But she couldn't be seduced. She couldn't forget for a minute that he wasn't a man who stayed in one place.

"Please put me down," she murmured.

Slowly he set her on the floor. "You're not going to pretend that didn't happen, are you?"

Oh, it had happened all right. She had even asked for it. "No, but..."

"I knew there was going to be a 'but,'" he grumbled.

"We're different, you and I."

"That's probably why we like each other," he said with half a smile.

"Maybe. Maybe you're exciting to me because you've been so many places. But excitement doesn't last and I believe in…commitment. I was raised to believe that a man and woman shouldn't…well, you know, before marriage."

"You and your husband didn't?"

"No." Her voice was firm. She had wondered all during her marriage if Pete had married her only for sex. He'd sure never acted like he wanted to be married. She'd been so wrong about him, and his lack of caring for her and Mark had hurt.

Slade ran his hand through his hair. "I see. So you're saying, unless I have serious intentions, I should stay away from you."

After thinking over his words for a moment, she replied, "I'm not ready for serious intentions. I'm not ready for anything that's going to complicate my life more than this ranch and my children already do." She hesitated. In spite of what she'd just said and what she believed, she did want Slade to stay. Telling herself the attraction between them could easily be pushed to the background if they both tried, she suggested, "But my life has plenty of room for a friend, Slade."

He seemed to think that over. "I don't think a man and a woman can be just friends if there's something in the air between them. But we can give it a try if that's what you want."

She thought about her friendship with Dallas, how it had always been comfortable, never complicated. But then she hadn't been attracted to him as she was to Slade. "That's what I want."

Slade's gaze searched her face and came to rest on her lips. It lingered there a few moments. The air between them was rife with the attraction they were both trying to push aside.

Emily took a deep breath. "I'm going to turn in now." It seemed essential that she move away from Slade, that she closet herself away in her room, that she forget about the lingering effects of his kiss.

Because if she didn't, they could never be friends.

The social hall attached to the church overflowed with people on Saturday morning. It was the first time Emily had been out with her baby daughter. She'd planned to make it a short trip to deliver the pies and say hello to a few people she rarely saw except for on occasions like these. Practically as soon as she entered the social hall, a group of women neighbors surrounded her, hoping to get a glimpse of the baby.

"I heard you named her Amanda," one said.

"And you had her alongside the road," another remarked.

Yet a third added, "And there's gossip that a man's living with you—"

At that moment, Slade came through the door carrying a box of pies. As usual, Mark was at his heels, feeling important by carrying a pie himself.

The women stopped talking and started looking when they saw Mark with Slade. One of them eyed Slade up and down, another frowned, and the third looked to Emily for an explanation.

But before Emily could even try to explain, Slade tipped his hat to them. "Morning, ladies. Emily, where would you like these?"

At the moment, she wished she'd never baked the pies. "Uh, back in the kitchen will be fine."

There was amusement in Slade's eyes as he saw

he was the object of everyone's attention. He headed in the direction of the kitchen.

"So it's true," the oldest of the three ranchers' wives said solemnly.

Cradling her daughter, Emily squared her shoulders. "I'm not sure what you've heard. Fortunately for me and Mark, Mr. Coleburn happened by before I went into labor. When labor did start, we couldn't make it to the hospital in time and he delivered Amanda by the side of the road in the van. I owe him her life and possibly more. He's staying on until I can handle all the chores myself again."

"But where is he staying?" Grace Harrison asked. She, her husband, son and daughter-in-law lived about ten miles from Emily on an adjoining spread.

Emily knew she couldn't keep secrets around these people. Somehow word always got out and it was better to be straightforward. "He's staying in Dad's room. I don't know what I would have done without him since Amanda was born."

Grace turned toward the kitchen. Emily saw Slade crouched down in front of Mark, working the zipper on his jacket. They were both laughing about something.

"It looks as if he and Mark get along just fine," Grace commented, her brows arched.

"They do," Emily said simply without elaborating.

"But he's not staying?" Flo Jansen asked.

"No. He's just passing through."

The three women exchanged looks, but Emily refused to feel embarrassed or ashamed. She nodded toward the tables that were filled with everything from embroidered baby bibs to jars of apple butter. "I'm going to take a look around while I'm here and see what everyone brought. Then I need to get Amanda home."

Moving away from the women, she felt their gazes on her back, and she tried to shrug off the feeling that she'd done something terribly wrong.

As she examined a baby bib with a colt embroidered on the front, the hairs on her nape prickled. Suddenly Slade was beside her, leaning close. "Do they want to ride me out on a rail?"

"It's not funny, Slade." Her voice quivered slightly.

"Emily…"

But when he placed his hand on her shoulder, she shrugged away. "We'd better go."

His mouth set in a tight line for a moment, and then he responded, "Fine. I'll round up Mark and meet you at the door."

Tears burned in Emily's eyes, and she looked down at her baby girl and gently brushed her finger along her chin. "It'll be all right, Amanda. Everything will be all right."

And she told herself it was so as she crossed to the door of the social hall, wishing she didn't care what anybody else thought, wishing she knew what she truly wanted.

Chapter Six

Two weeks before Christmas, Slade came into the house at lunch time after handling a morning full of chores. The scent of cinnamon and something good baking filled his nostrils. Emily was at the sink slicing carrots into a bowl. She was wearing jeans and a blouse with long sleeves that buttoned down the front, and she'd never looked prettier. But, then, he thought that every day. There had been a strain between them ever since that morning after Thanksgiving in the social hall. They hadn't spoken about it, but Slade guessed Emily didn't like being the butt of gossip. The thing was—if there was nothing happening between them, she had no cause to feel guilty about him living there.

But they both knew something *was* between them and that was the problem.

She glanced at him as he hung up his jacket and hat.

"Something smells good," he said casually. He

How To Play:

No Risk!

1. With a coin, carefully scratch off the 3 gold areas on your Lucky Carnival Wheel. By doing so you have qualified to receive everything revealed — 2 FREE books and a surprise gift — ABSOLUTELY FREE!

2. Send back this card and you'll receive brand-new Silhouette Romance® novels. These books have a cover price of $3.50 each in the U.S. and $3.99 each in Canada, but they are yours TOTALLY FREE!

3. There's no catch! You're under no obligation to buy anything. We charge nothing — ZERO — for your first shipment. And you don't have to make any minimum number of purchases—not even one!

4. The fact is thousands of readers enjoy receiving books by mail from the Silhouette Reader Service™. They enjoy the convenience of home delivery...they like getting the best new novels at discount prices, BEFORE they're available in stores...and they love their *Heart to Heart* subscriber newsletter featuring author news, horoscopes, recipes, book reviews and much more!

5. We hope that after receiving your free books you'll want to remain a subscriber. But the choice is yours — to continue or cancel, anytime at all! So why not take us up on our invitation, with no risk of any kind. You'll be glad you did.

No Cost!

LUCKY
Find Out Instantly The Gifts You Get
Absolutely FREE!
Carnival Wheel
Scratch-off Game

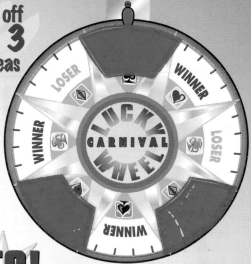

Scratch off ALL 3 Gold areas

YES!
I have scratched off the 3 Gold Areas above. Please send me the 2 FREE books and gift for which I qualify! I understand I am under no obligation to purchase any books, as explained on the back and on the opposite page.

315 SDL CY4K   215 SDL CY4F

NAME   (PLEASE PRINT CLEARLY)

ADDRESS

APT.#   CITY

STATE/PROV.   ZIP/POSTAL CODE

▶ DETACH AND MAIL CARD TODAY! ▶

The Silhouette Reader Service™ — Here's how it works:

Accepting your 2 free books and gift places you under no obligation to buy anything. You may keep the books and gift and return the shipping statement marked "cancel." If you do not cancel, about a month later we'll send you 6 additional novels and bill you just $2.90 each in the U.S., or $3.25 each in Canada, plus 25¢ delivery per book and applicable taxes if any.* That's the complete price and — compared to cover prices of $3.50 each in the U.S. and $3.99 each in Canada — it's quite a bargain! You may cancel at any time, but if you choose to continue, every month we'll send you 6 more books, which you may either purchase at the discount price or return to us and cancel your subscription.

*Terms and prices subject to change without notice. Sales tax applicable in N.Y. Canadian residents will be charged applicable provincial taxes and GST.

tried to keep everything casual between them lately, but that was damn hard. Especially when she looked at him with soft brown eyes that knew better.

"I made bread pudding. It'll come out of the oven any minute now. Mail came for you." She nodded to the table where an envelope sat propped against the salt and pepper shakers.

Mail? An answer to one of his ads? His heart began pounding. Picking it up, he pulled out a kitchen chair and sat, just staring at the envelope a few moments. A return address was hastily scrawled. John Morgan from Denver.

"Slade? What is it?" Emily asked gently.

"I almost don't want to know," he murmured. "This could be something that will change my life forever no matter what it is."

"The only way you'll find out is to open it," she urged quietly.

At first Slade wondered if maybe he should do this in private, but then he realized he was glad Emily was here. Tearing open the envelope, he slid out the letter, then unfolded it. As he read, his heart beat faster, and after he finished, he looked up at Emily, his throat tight. He cleared it. "This man in Denver says he and his wife adopted a child over thirty-one years ago. The boy's name was Hunter Coleburn. They were living in Tucson at the time, but moved to Billings soon after. Eventually they moved to Denver."

"Does he say where Hunter is now?" Emily asked.

"Hunter's an international corporate attorney and he's out of the country." Slade stared down at the letter again. The information he'd just given Emily hung in the air between them.

"Are you leaving for Denver?" she asked.

Two more weeks and it would be Christmas. Slade knew he shouldn't feel held to this place. He'd never felt held to any place. Yet, Hunter Coleburn wasn't even in the country. Why go on a wild-goose chase when Emily needed him? Because she did even if she wouldn't admit it.

"There are cattle and horses to tend and more snow coming. This can wait." Slipping the letter into its envelope, he stuffed it into his shirt pocket.

"How long have you wanted family, Slade?"

The look in Emily's eyes said she wouldn't let him evade her. "I've never had it, so I don't know if I want it."

"You don't want to meet your brother?"

"I don't know if he *is* my brother. And even if he is, he's out of the country."

"But if you went and talked to these people—"

"I thought you said Mark wanted me here for the holidays."

"He does, but we're not your real family, Slade. And I don't want to be responsible for you not finding Hunter."

"I didn't say I wasn't going to find him. I'll write back to this John Morgan and send him a picture. If Hunter and I are twins, he'll be able to tell me that. And if this is some coincidence, I'll find that out, too. Either way, I'll be here for Christmas. Unless you really want me to leave. If the gossip's getting to you, if you think you're doing something wrong…"

"I'm not doing anything wrong."

"Then stop acting as if you are. Stop acting as if our gazes shouldn't meet and our fingers shouldn't touch and we shouldn't spend time together now and then."

Her cheeks flushed and he realized he'd hit all the nails on their heads.

"It's not as if we've had much time to spend together," she murmured.

"A family and a ranch eat up time," he agreed. "But if we really wanted to find a little, I imagine we could. In fact, I want to go into town to do some Christmas shopping. Maybe Mavis could watch Amanda and you could go with me while Mark's in school."

He wished Emily didn't look so uncertain. He wished he could dream about the future. But he'd learned long ago that dreams were wisps of life, imaginings that could make a boy hurt and yearn. Like smoke, the wisps disappeared and could leave a boy or a man alone with reality of this world, not the one he wished for.

Waiting, he almost expected Emily to refuse his offer.

The bell went off on the timer. She broke eye contact, opened the oven door, then reached for two pot holders and took out the bread pudding. Its wonderful smell became even more alive and so did his desire for Emily.

Finally she laid the pot holders on the counter and brushed her hair away from her face, meeting his gaze once more. "I do have some shopping to do."

"How long can you leave Amanda? I'd like to take you to lunch."

"I can express milk and work with her on taking

a bottle. It's a good thing to do in case of emergencies anyway. Then we won't have to worry about what time we get back."

He couldn't keep the grin from stealing across his face and he stood, going to her. "We could call this a date," he teased.

"We're going shopping, Slade."

"Then I guess it will be a shopping date."

She shook her head. "Sometimes you're..."

Slipping his thumb under her chin, he tipped it up. "Sometimes I'm what?"

But she didn't answer him. Staying away from her, trying not to want her, was just too damn difficult. As she went perfectly still and stared up at him, he lowered his head and his lips covered hers. The kiss seemed to stretch into next year as the taste of her made him hungrier, the sensuality of her made him needier. The pure temptation of her almost made him believe in a dream. She melted into his arms and kissed him back with an abandon that surprised him. But he knew it would be better to leave her wanting more. It would be better for him to stop this before she did, before her thoughts got tangled up in the desire and she convinced herself she should stay away from him again. Slowing things down, he loosened his hold on her, stopped the mating of his tongue with hers and slowly withdrew.

When she looked up at him, she looked bemused and he figured that was a good way to leave it.

"I'm going to go wash up," he said, trying to keep his voice from being low and husky. "Just holler when lunch is ready."

And before she had the chance to tell him that they shouldn't do that again, that they shouldn't go shopping together, that he shouldn't consider it a date, he went down the hall to the bathroom with a smile on his face.

After Slade and Emily shopped separately for a short while at a small mall on the outskirts of Billings, they met up at the toy store. It was a wonderland of lost wishes for Slade. It held everything he'd always wanted as a boy and could never have—balls and gloves and trucks and games. They'd had mostly leftovers at the home in Tucson. Things people had used too hard or didn't want anymore. Rarely new. And he'd never had to buy Christmas presents for people before. It had been years since he'd received a present let alone given one. But this year he wanted to give. He needed to give.

He knew Emily wouldn't accept much. Through the years to pass time, he'd begun carving. For the last two weeks, he'd been working on a fawn for Emily. He was pretty sure she'd like it but could never be completely certain about her reactions.

But Mark was a different matter entirely.

As they walked down a row stocked with stuffed animals, Slade said to Emily, "I thought about getting Mark a saddle for Christmas. One that fits him."

She stopped. "Mark doesn't need a new saddle. He uses mine."

"And when the two of you go riding?"

"We manage. I use Pete's old saddle."

"It wouldn't hurt for Mark to have one of his own, to hold onto for years to come."

Her gaze was troubled when she looked up at

him. "That's a gift that's much too expensive, Slade. I can't let you do that."

"It seems to me gifts shouldn't have tags on them that say too-much-or-too-little." Emily started walking again and Slade knew this was going to be an uphill battle. He asked, "What are you getting Mark?"

"Mavis found me a sled at a sale. It just needs a good coat of paint. And I want to get him a new baseball and bat. Come spring he'll play on a team at school."

"What about a glove?"

Emily shook her head and Slade suspected a glove wouldn't fit into her budget.

As they approached the rack of balls and gloves and other sports equipment, Slade stopped. "Let me buy him a glove, a football and maybe a basketball. You have the perfect place beside the barn where he could shoot hoops."

"Slade…"

He knew a lecture was coming and he didn't want to hear it. "Christmas is a time for toys, and for kids getting what they want, not being deprived."

"I don't think Mark feels deprived. I've always given him everything I can. And there's Amanda now, too."

"All the more reason to let me give him something special," Slade concluded. "If not a saddle, how about a wagon or a bicycle?"

"Do you want to do this so he remembers you after you're gone?" Emily asked.

Maybe he did. Maybe he wanted to feel as if he'd left some mark on the boy or given Mark something to remember him by. But he didn't like her pointing it out. "I just think Mark needs to know he's special, that he's not any different from any other kid. You can think about the bike or the wagon and I'll abide by your decision on that. But I'm buying him a few balls and the glove, at least."

The checkout counter was busy even though it was midday. Christmas was getting close. Emily peeked glances at Slade every now and then as they went through the line. She knew that determined set of his jaw. She knew how remote he could become when his eyes turned that color of blue, sort of like a stormy sky, and she guessed giving presents to Mark was important to him for more than one reason.

As they came out of the store and put bags and boxes in the back of the van, snow started to fall. Slade looked up and frowned. "I hope it doesn't get too heavy. I wanted to take Mark to cut down a Christmas tree either today or tomorrow when he gets home from school. Or do you have something against Christmas trees?"

Trying to keep her temper in check, she stepped back. "I'm not Scrooge, Slade. I've just learned how to make do on a shoestring."

He looked chagrined for a moment and then slammed the back door into place. She motioned to a corner of the parking lot where a display was set up with lighted trees and small mechanical figures of animals and children. "Do you want to walk and take a look before we get lunch?"

"You'll be cold," he muttered.

"I'll be fine. I can bundle up since I fit into my coat again," she said with a smile.

But he didn't smile in return, just waited for her to start walking with him toward the lighted trees.

Although snow was falling, there was almost no wind and Emily enjoyed stretching her legs, being outside, being with Slade. When they reached the fenced-in display, they gazed at the little train circling a tree, the figures of animals and children. "Tell me about Christmas when you were a boy," Emily suggested.

The intensity of Slade's look should have made her turn away, but she didn't. She simply waited.

He was silent for so long she thought he wasn't going to speak, but then he confessed, "Christmas was always a disappointment. All of us lived at the home, but we went to school with normal kids and there was this big buildup before Christmas. Kids constantly talked about what they were getting, what they wanted, what Santa Claus would bring. Yet any of us who lived at the home knew there was no Santa Claus. Hell, we didn't even have parents, let alone believe in somebody in a red suit who would bring us presents. And it's not that I'm ungrateful for what they did for us. They kept us warm, they fed us, they gave us the care they could. On Christmas we got an orange, a candy cane, one present, usually a puzzle. Like you said, life on a shoestring is tough. The home had to watch costs wherever they could."

Emily gently clasped his arm. "Christmas isn't about gifts or shiny paper and fancy bows. It isn't that I don't want Mark to have the things you want to give him. But I want him to realize he can be happy without them."

"Oh, Emily." Slade shook his head. "I know

you're right, but yet I know how I felt as a kid. I got back to school after the holidays and kids with families would talk about relatives staying and gifts they'd brought and shiny new bikes and wagons and electric trains. It was another world, and it was as if I didn't belong in it or didn't have a right to it, or didn't deserve it."

Stepping closer to him, Emily looked straight into his eyes. "You deserve happiness, Slade, and a family and people who care about you." Suddenly she realized how much she cared about him. She'd bought him a book earlier, and though she hadn't had much spare time lately, when he was out doing chores, she'd started knitting him a pair of socks. It wouldn't be much, but there was caring in each stitch and now she realized it was more than caring. Caring was turning to love. She'd tried to guard against it, but something about Slade had stolen into her and wrapped around her heart.

Still, she could prevent herself from becoming more deeply involved. She could prevent her heart from being broken when he left.

His eyes changed from stormy to deep, deep blue and she knew they'd better get to lunch or he'd be kissing her and she'd be forgetting she had to keep her heart safe. Releasing his arm, she wrapped hers around herself. "You were right, it is cold out here, even though I'm bundled up. I guess we'd better get some lunch."

He smiled at her then. "Lunch it is. Anything on the menu your heart desires."

When she glanced over at the placard on the family-style restaurant, she knew she wouldn't find what her heart desired on that menu. But she knew exactly what it was. And it scared her.

The excitement of seeing Christmas shine in Mark's eyes was everything to Slade as they bumped along the rutted snow tracks to a stand of firs. Thinking about yesterday and the near argument with Emily in the toy store, he realized cutting down a Christmas tree with Mark would be important to them both. Emily put the emphasis on tradition and intangibles of holidays. He'd try to abide by that as best he could.

Today had been clear and bright, not filled with clouds and snow as yesterday had. But they had less than an hour of daylight left so they'd have to move quickly. Slade parked along the barbed-wire fence and saw he'd have to lift Mark over it. The snow had mounded and there wasn't enough room for the boy to crawl under.

"Mom told me Gramps used to cut down our Christmas trees," Mark said as Slade reached for his seat belt.

"What about after your gramps died?"

"Mom would just cut down a small one and bring it in. But we couldn't fit much on that. Can we get a really big one?"

Slade laughed. "Only as tall as the ceiling. I don't think your mom would let us cut a hole in the floor above."

Mark giggled and they both jumped out of the truck.

As they trudged through the snow, Mark asked, "Will you be here after Christmas?"

"Any special reason you're asking?" Slade asked, figuring Mark had something in mind.

"There's gonna be a Fun Festival at school after New Year's. Kids and their dads build a snowman if we can go outside. The best one wins a prize. And there's games in the gym. I was wonderin'…if you could go with me."

From the look in Mark's eyes, Slade saw this was important to him. "Sure, I can go with you. I haven't built a snowman in a while, but I imagine you could help me practice if the weather holds out."

Mark grinned and vigorously bobbed his head. "Sure."

Slade wasn't used to having anyone look up to him. It made him uncomfortable but also kind of good. Clasping Mark's shoulder, he said, "But, right now, we have to pick out a tree."

When they reached the fence, it was easy to lift Mark over it. Then Slade grabbed the saw and stepped over the barbed wire himself. The snow was deeper out here than back at the house and it took them longer than Slade expected to reach the trees and find the right one. Apparently Mark not only wanted a tall tree, but a perfect tree, one with no holes, plenty of branches and a nice straight trunk. Slade seconded the straight trunk. But by the time they both found one they decided was just right, the sun was slipping below the horizon.

"We'll have to hurry," Slade joked, "or we'll need the moon to guide us."

"I'm glad you're going to be here for Christmas," Mark said, looking up at him with big brown eyes, red cheeks and a worshipful smile.

A lump lodged in Slade's throat and he realized

how much this little boy was coming to mean to him. "I'm glad I'm going to be here, too. Now come on, we've got to get a move on."

It was dark by the time they cut down the tree and Slade dragged it to the fence. Slade laid down the tree and the saw. "Come here, partner. I'll lift you over."

Mark held up his arms and Slade transferred the boy to the other side. "Go get in the truck so you keep warm."

As Mark scurried off, Slade picked up the saw and tossed it down on the other side of the fence, then he lifted the eight-foot tree and climbed over the barbed wire. But in the darkness he misjudged, and the weight of the tree took him over faster than he expected. The side of his thigh brushed against the barbed wire. He could hear the tear of his jeans, and he felt the stings. Cursing and deciding it was his own fault for hurrying, he ignored the cuts, carried the tree to the back of the pickup, heaving it into the payload. After he fetched the saw, he tossed it back there, too, then climbed into the truck.

"All set?" he asked Mark, deciding his leg had simply gotten scratched.

"I'm ready for supper," the seven-year-old said enthusiastically. "Are we going to trim the tree tonight?"

"We'll have to talk to your mom about that, but I don't see why not."

Emily had left the tree-stand out on the front porch. Slade shooed Mark inside before he shaped the trunk with the saw and secured it in the stand. Then he opened the kitchen door. "Are you ready to put the tree in the living room?" he called inside.

Emily was taking a roast out of the oven and she smiled at him. "I rearranged things a little and we're ready. Bring it in."

Hoisting the tree into his arms, he carried it into the living room. Amanda was sleeping in her cradle by the armchair. He saw the place Emily had made for the tree in front of the window. It seemed to take up at least half the room.

"I guess Mark wanted a big tree this year," she said with a smile.

"And perfect all the way around."

Standing back, she pretended to examine it carefully. She'd looked it up and down and was about to say something, when her gaze fell on Slade's leg. "Goodness, what did you do?"

When he looked down, he saw there were several tears in his jeans and they were matted with blood. He was sure it looked worse than it was. "It's just a few scratches. The barbed wire and I had a tussle."

"You'd better let me see to that. Have you had a tetanus shot lately?"

"Last summer."

"That's a relief. Come down to the bathroom and we'll clean it up."

"Emily, really…"

"You'd better do it Slade so it doesn't get infected," Mark warned him, and Slade knew the boy had probably heard those words many times from his mother.

"I don't want to hold up supper," he groused.

"Supper will keep for a few minutes. Mark, how about if you go upstairs and get washed up. I'll take care of Slade down here."

In other circumstances, Slade might rejoice at Emily's words, but not in these particular ones. She followed him down the hall to the bathroom and once inside they both realized how small the quarters were. When neither of them moved, she finally said, "You'll have to take your pants off."

He searched his mind for a smart comeback, but damn, he couldn't find one. "Emily…"

Her cheeks were flushed as she opened the medicine cabinet, reached inside and took out a bottle of peroxide. "We'll be done before you know it. You've got to be a good example for Mark."

He wasn't sure what kind of example he'd be with his pants off. "I'll take care of it myself," he muttered.

"It's at a bad spot and hard to reach. It'll be easier for me to do it."

Not easier on his nerves or on the desire he already felt stirring. When his hands went to his belt buckle, Emily was still fussing around the medicine cabinet, but her cheeks were getting even rosier. He figured the best thing to do was get this over as quickly as possible. She had him so flustered he forgot he had to take his foot out of his boot before he could get the pants leg off. Stooping down, he yanked off the boot and tossed it into the hall. Slipping one leg out of his jeans, he left the other leg on. The material of the jeans had stuck in spots to the wounds and now they started bleeding again.

"Oh, Slade, that's got to hurt."

"Nope. Didn't know it was there."

She rolled her eyes and shook her head and picked up a soft, clean cloth that she rinsed, then sudsed with a translucent looking soap. "This is antibacterial. It'll clean the wounds before I put the peroxide on. That'll go deeper.''

"Pleasant thought," he muttered. "Let's just get this done."

Although she was as quick and efficient as a nurse, he was still very aware of every touch of her fingers on his skin. He could imagine them other places…as they lay in bed…. When he realized the effect his thoughts were having, he tried to stop them. But stopping them was as difficult as keeping his distance, as not wanting to kiss Emily again and again. Her head was bent as she tended to his leg. The yellow light in the bathroom picked up the blond strands in her hair. He knew it was soft and silky. He knew if he touched it, he wouldn't want to stop.

After she'd finished with the soap and peroxide, she used a cream and, despite the scratches stinging on his leg, the softness of her touch, the sweet torture of her fingers on the back of his thigh, were enough to make him want to groan. No way could he face her. No way could he let her see…

She applied a gauze bandage much too fast and, if he didn't want to be rude and keep his back to her, he had no choice but to turn and look at her, holding his jeans up as best he could to disguise what was happening to him.

But before he could put his other leg in his pants and escape to his room, she said, "Why don't you just take them off altogether. I'll wash them then see if I can repair them."

"That's not necessary."

"It will be when you need a pair of clean jeans."

Damn if she wasn't going to stand here and argue with him.

But it wasn't arguing that made his blood rush faster when her gaze shifted from his leg and inadvertently rested near his belt buckle. He was aroused and there was no way to hide it.

Her cheeks became almost red as she quickly turned away from him and stowed the bandages and tape in the medicine cabinet.

Stepping into his pants, zipping and fastening them quickly, he came up behind her and put his hands on her shoulders. "Don't be embarrassed, Emily. I think you know how I feel about you without seeing the proof of it."

Finally she met his gaze in the mirror. "I *am* embarrassed. I should have realized—"

Turning her toward him, he gently stroked her hair from her face. "No matter what my reactions are to you, you know you have nothing to fear, don't you?"

"I'm not afraid of you," she answered him.

Yet there was something in her voice, something that made him wonder what sex had been like between her and her husband. "But?" he prompted.

"But men's needs and women's needs are a lot different."

"How so?"

"A man's needs are all physical. A woman's needs are a lot more complicated."

"I'm not going to tell you my reaction to you isn't physical, but there's more to it than that. You've given me something here I've never had before. Meaning in the holidays...traditions. And I appreciate that. What's between us isn't just physical, though I think you're afraid of both what is *and* what isn't.''

Her chin went up. "I'm not afraid."

Cocking his head, he gave her a slow smile. "What would you call it?"

"I'm cautious, and I have to be. When you're gone, I'll still have the same life I've always had. I'll still have two children to care for and a ranch to run, though I'm not sure how much longer I can do that. Kissing you might be pleasurable, but I can't let it distract me from what's really important.''

To him, the desire he felt for Emily, the sense of rightness being in her presence was much more than pleasurable. But she was right about it being fleeting. Still, if he didn't have a brother to find, he might stay longer…but that didn't mean she'd want him to or that anything would be any different than it was now.

When he heard footsteps running down the hall, Slade stepped away from her.

Mark burst into the doorway. "I'm all washed up and Amanda's crying. Are we going to eat now?"

Emily looked flustered, but she stepped out of the bathroom into the hall. "Can you try to distract your sister while I get supper out? Then I'll feed her while you and Slade get started.''

"Sure. Is Slade's leg gonna be okay?"

She looked down at where the white patches showed through the torn jeans.

But Slade was the one who answered. "It's going to be just fine, Mark." He wished he could say the same about the emptiness he felt inside when he thought about leaving. He wished he could say the same about his feelings toward Emily and her children. But he'd always been a "take one day at a time" kind of guy and there was no reason to change that philosophy now.

Chapter Seven

Boxes of Christmas decorations strayed across the living-room floor as Emily steadied Mark on a step stool so he could hang a miniature bell up high. As she glanced over at Slade who was standing at her side examining a shiny blue ball with Mark's name written on it, she felt her cheeks get hot all over again. No man had ever made her feel as he did, all tingly and weak-kneed. Especially standing this close, she was aware of his body heat, his scent, his long legs, his...

When she'd glimpsed his arousal earlier in the bathroom, she'd felt excited and aroused herself, and now she wondered what would happen if she gave in to the feelings. Really gave into them. In a couple of weeks she could think about—

In a couple of weeks, Slade might be gone.

"Can I put the star on top before I go to bed?" Mark asked.

Even when they'd simply cut a small tree, they'd

put the star on top. "Sure you can. But the step stool won't be high enough for that."

"I'll lift you up," Slade said.

She moved away from him. "The star's in the box by the sofa."

Mark jumped from the stool and went to find it.

Lifting the ball in his hand, Slade asked her, "Did you paint this?" Mark's name, birth date and a small angel decorated the ornament.

"For his first Christmas."

"You know how to make things matter."

Slade's voice, low and deep, made her insides tremble. "What do you mean?"

"Mark thinks he's special every time he looks at this. I'll bet you bake him a birthday cake every year, too, don't you?"

She nodded, willing to bet Slade never had a celebration for his birthday. "When's your birthday?" she asked.

"April 8th."

She suspected he'd be long gone by then.

Changing the subject, Slade pointed to a crocheted snowflake she'd hung on the tree. "Some of these ornaments look old."

"My mother made that when I was five. Many of these hung on our tree when I was little. Mark likes to hear the stories behind them, where they came from." She pointed to a bucking bronc fashioned from metal. "Dad bought that one when he visited a friend in Wyoming." And carefully she tapped a tiny wooden church. "That one Dallas gave me when we were in high school. They all have memories attached."

With Slade looking down at her very seriously,

she wondered what was going through his head until he said, "I never realized Christmas trees are memory trees. It must be nice to have all those good memories. They must make you feel...connected."

She wanted to say, *You could be connected, too.*

But before the thought could be put into words, Mark came over to them with the star. "Here it is."

Slade hung Mark's ornament on the tree and lifted the boy so he could slip the wire attached to the star over the tall treetop. It was gold and a little tarnished, but Mark looked up at it in awe as if it was the most beautiful star on earth.

After Slade set him down, her son looked up at her. "Doesn't it look great way up there? Didn't we pick out the *best* tree?"

"The absolute best tree." She smiled at Slade because he'd made this moment possible, because he was making this Christmas special for Mark by being here.

And for you, too, a small voice whispered. But she tried to ignore it.

"Can we light it up?" Mark asked.

She only had one string of lights that worked but they would add sparkle to the tree. "We'll light it and then you can get your pj's on."

"Can we sing a Christmas carol?"

Emily turned to Slade to explain. "We usually do that after we light the tree."

"Another tradition?" he asked, his voice husky. She nodded.

After Slade plugged in the lights, Emily put her arm around Mark. "What do you want to sing?"

"Silent Night," he answered without hesitating.

After Emily started the song, Mark joined in, and

then finally Slade. When they finished, they were all quiet, savoring the moment Emily knew would last a lifetime.

But then the phone rang, breaking the silence. Emily picked up the baby monitor on the end table and went to answer the phone, saying to Mark, "Go ahead upstairs. I'll be up when I finish."

The evening had been a turbulent one for Slade, and after he said good-night to Mark, he followed Emily to the kitchen intent on going to his room. He'd never been involved in family traditions before. He'd never cut down a Christmas tree or watched Christmas come alive in a child's eyes. Tonight when they'd plugged in the tree lights, he'd gotten a lump in his throat that he couldn't dislodge. His chest had felt tight, and when he'd finally joined in the singing, the chaos inside him made him realize that maybe he'd stayed at the Double Blaze too long already. What was he doing here when he didn't belong? What was he doing here acting at times as if he was one of the family?

He would have gone to his room to sort his thoughts but then he heard Emily greet the caller on the phone. "Hi, Dallas. Are you home for Christmas already?"

Suddenly Slade needed a glass of milk, and he was going to take his time about getting it. Listening unabashedly, he found out Dallas was still at the university. Even only hearing one side of the conversation, he guessed the man was checking up on Emily, making sure she and Mark didn't need anything, making sure she was safe from a stranger who might harm her.

Once she glanced over at Slade and said, "Yes,

he's still here. He'll be staying through the holidays.''

A few minutes later as Slade stood at the counter and drank his milk slowly, Emily hung up the phone.

He set down his glass and asked casually, ''Did Dallas want anything special?''

''Not really. He was just checking in. Neighbors look after neighbors out here. Wasn't it that way on other ranches where you worked?''

''On those other ranches, I lived in the bunkhouse. I didn't particularly know what was going on with the people who lived there. I just did my work. Don't you think Dallas is pretty far away to be neighborly?''

''Distance doesn't interfere with friendship. After Pete died, Dallas started calling every couple of weeks. He just wants to make sure I'm okay,'' she added quietly.

Their eyes met.

''How's your leg?'' Emily asked.

''Fine.''

''You wouldn't tell me if it wasn't, would you?''

Her tone was accusing, and he realized it felt kind of nice to have her fussing over him. He gave her a slow smile. ''I wouldn't want to spoil my tough cowboy image.''

His gentle teasing brought her a few steps closer to him. ''You've got a good heart, Slade. You're making this Christmas special for Mark.''

''You're wrong there. You and your kids are making it special for me. I never had a Christmas that I really wanted to celebrate before.'' He paused, then went on. ''I was taking a look at that sled you got. Since you nixed the idea of a bicycle or a wagon, how about if I sand it down for you. We'll make it a joint project.''

"Well," she said slowly, pretending to think about it. "Only if you promise to let me throw that football around with you and Mark out in the snow after he opens it.''

He had a hard time imagining Emily playing football, but tackling her could be a heck of a lot of fun. "The more the merrier," he agreed with a chuckle.

And then they gazed into each other's eyes again, aware of the electricity pulling them together, aware of a bond growing between them even if neither of them wanted it. He wanted to kiss her so badly. Everything in him shouted to take her in his arms. But he wasn't sure he could stop with a kiss anymore. He wasn't sure he could keep a kiss simple. He wasn't sure he should stay even a day after Christmas.

Emily backed away from him. "I'd better get upstairs.''

Slade nodded to the baby monitor in her hand. "If you want to leave that while you put Mark to bed, I'll listen for Amanda. If she wakes up before you're finished, I'll distract her." He enjoyed holding the baby, but he didn't do it too often because he might get used to it.

When Emily handed him the monitor, their fingers brushed, and neither of them pulled away. He could see in her brown eyes some of the emotion he was feeling. But he chalked it up to the sentimentality of the holidays. He chalked it up to feeling as if he were part of a family when he never had been before.

As Emily went upstairs, he thought about his real family, the brother he hadn't found yet, and the difference Hunter Coleburn could make in his life.

On the day before Christmas, Slade had just returned from checking on cattle when Mark came running toward the corral. Out of breath, the boy said, "Come quick. Mom says you got an important phone call."

Only one person had Slade's number here, John Morgan, Hunter Coleburn's adoptive father. Turning loose the horse he'd ridden into the corral, Slade hurried to the house, Mark running beside him trying to keep up. Coming inside, Mark slammed the door behind him. Emily didn't scold, but just pointed to the receiver on the counter and said to Slade, "It's Hunter Coleburn."

Then his heart began thudding.

Draping her arm around her son's shoulders, Emily said to Mark, "Let's go into the living room and let Slade have some privacy."

Slade waited until they were in the next room. "Hello?"

"Slade Coleburn?" a deep voice asked.

"Yes."

"This is Hunter Coleburn. I just returned to my office in London and found a message from my parents. After we talked, they faxed me your letter and the picture you enclosed. Except for the fact that I have black hair, and my father tells me in the picture yours is brown, we could pass for each other. We're twins, Slade."

With Slade's heart hammering in his chest, he didn't know what to say next, and he couldn't tell from Hunter's tone what the man thought about finding a lost brother. "What do you think about all of it?"

There was silence at the other end of the line. "It's a shock. I didn't know I had any family. Real family. I didn't think..." He stopped. "This is hard to discuss over the phone, and I won't be back in the country for at least another three weeks. I'd like to see you then. Maybe you could come to Denver or I can fly to Montana."

"We can talk about it when you get back to the States," Slade assured him. "I'm not sure I'll still be here then, but I'll contact you if I'm not. Can you give me a number where I can reach you?"

Hunter did, and Slade jotted it down on the notepad beside the phone. Afterward, particularly curious about something, he asked, "Is there a reason you kept the Coleburn name?"

"It was my middle name until I was twenty-one, then I decided to reclaim it."

Slade suspected there was a lot Hunter wasn't saying, but they'd need more than a five-minute conversation to get to know each other. It might take the rest of their lives.

As if thinking the same thing, Hunter asked, "Dad said you were working on a ranch in Montana. Is that what you do?"

"I do a little bit of everything. I've worked construction jobs, but I like the wide-open spaces. I've moved around a lot. What about you?"

"My specialty is international law, so I often travel. It seems as if we both have the urge to...roam."

There was more silence as if the two men didn't

know where to begin. Finally Slade said, "I'm glad you called. I'm not sure if I ever really expected to find you."

"I'm glad you did. I'll be in touch when I can be more definite about my plans."

"Sounds good. I'll keep you informed where you can reach me. You have a good Christmas."

"It's already good," Hunter murmured, his voice going deeper. "Take care. I'll call you soon."

When Slade hung up the phone, his throat was tight. He heard Mark as the boy ran up the stairs and he wondered if Emily had sent him for something.

She came into the kitchen carrying Amanda, holding the baby on her shoulder. "Do you want to talk about it?" she asked gently as she patted Amanda's back.

He'd never had anyone to talk things over with before and had never really seen the need. A man handled his own problems. A man followed his own good sense and had to find his own answers. Yet Hunter Coleburn wasn't a problem, and there were no answers to seek, at least not yet.

"I do have a twin. Hunter's father faxed him my picture and he says we look alike."

Tilting her head, Emily studied him. "How does it feel to have a brother?"

"Odd. I mean I don't know what I expected. But it was like talking to a stranger."

"You *are* strangers. You *will* be until you spend some time together. Are you going to do that?"

"He seems to want to. So do I. But he's in London right now on business. He doesn't think he'll be back till the middle of January. So any reunion will have to wait.''

''What's he like?'' Emily asked.

''Reserved…educated. We probably don't have much in common.''

''You have blood in common. That's powerful, Slade.''

Amanda started squirming a bit on Emily's shoulder and for a distraction as much as anything else, Slade reached out and took her, cradling her in his arms, rocking her, thinking about the bond she had with her brother. Then he looked up at Emily, feeling the bond that was growing stronger with her. Since the night they'd decorated the tree, they'd been easier with each other. They were still backing away from the chemistry, but she didn't jerk away when he accidentally touched her, and he took every opportunity he could to get close to her. They'd had fun painting Mark's sled together. And he'd wrapped the gifts he'd bought for Mark one night, while she painted his name on the sled.

''Would you like to go to church with me tonight?'' she asked.

''Do you want to take the baby?''

''Mavis said she'd come over and sit with Mark and Amanda if I…if we…wanted to go.''

Slade doubted Mavis was doing it so he could take Emily to church, but he wouldn't look a gift horse in the mouth. ''I'd like to take you. Wouldn't Mark mind missing out?''

''He'll be in bed. The service isn't until ten-thirty. We should be home by midnight.''

Suddenly Slade thought about going to church, Emily's neighbors and the clothes he had with him.

But that could be easily fixed. "I have to run into town this afternoon. Do you need anything?"

She shook her head. "I have everything I need right now."

As he looked down at her, he thought, he did, too.

Getting Mark to bed on Christmas Eve took a little longer than usual. The boy was excited, there was no doubt about that, Slade thought, as he went to his room to get dressed for church. Emily had fed Amanda and the baby, too, was tucked in at least for the next couple of hours. Slade had just tugged on a new pair of black boots when he heard voices in the kitchen. He supposed Mavis had arrived. Taking his new Western-cut camel blazer from a hanger, he slipped it on, then walked down the hall to the kitchen.

When the two women saw him, they stopped talking and stared. Emily's gaze went from the top of his head to his string tie, white shirt and blazer, down the black jeans and boots. She was obviously at a loss for words.

Did he look so different out of his flannel shirt and blue jeans? She herself was as pretty as any picture in a russet long-sleeved dress with a flared skirt that came to the top of her boots.

With the women still staring at him, he rubbed his jaw and joked, "Did I miss a spot shaving?"

Emily blushed and Mavis laughed.

"Women can't help but stare at a man all spruced up for Christmas Eve," Mavis remarked with a smile.

"Is that true, Emily?" he teased.

"I, uh...you just look different."

"Different good or different bad?"

"I almost didn't know you."

"I'm the same man under the clothes, Emily."

Her cheeks grew even redder. "I suppose we should be going if we don't want to be late."

He decided to let her change the subject. "I'm ready when you are."

Lifting her coat from the kitchen chair, he held it for her. When she put one arm in, she was so close to him he could smell the scent of her shampoo, something flowery like the lotion she wore. When she slipped her other arm in, he didn't let go of the coat but fixed the lapel at her neck, brushing his fingers through the ends of her hair as if it were an accident.

She gazed over her shoulder at him, and he felt his heart skip.

He could hardly remember what he said to Mavis before they left. The whole way to church in the van, he kept glancing at Emily and she at him.

Finally she said, "You look very handsome tonight."

"I clean up well, do I?"

"Slade…"

"I can't help but tease you. You should have seen your face. I didn't know there was such a difference between wearing a coat and tie and a flannel shirt."

"It wasn't that."

"What was it?"

The wind blew against the van, the heater hummed, the stars above shone down on them.

"I thought I was coming to know you and then tonight, you looked so different, I wondered if I really *do* know you."

"You know me, Emily. What there is to know. Just because I went and bought some new duds doesn't mean I'm going to act any different. You don't act any different when you put lipstick on do you?"

She was wearing a natural shade tonight that blended well with the dress. "Actually I do," she said honestly. "Getting dressed up, putting lipstick on, makes me feel more...womanly."

He let a few heartbeats go by, then he murmured, "I'll remember that."

When they arrived at the church, the small parking lot was already full of cars. As they went inside, they saw most of the pews were full. A family made room for them at the end of a pew on the left side and, as Slade let Emily pass him to go in first, he saw some curious eyes on them. After he took his place facing forward, he spotted Dallas O'Neill two pews from the front. As far as Slade could tell, there was no one with him. No woman with him, that is.

It had been years since Slade attended a church service. The last time had been about five years ago at Easter. He'd gone with a couple of the hands on the ranch where he'd been working. But tonight there was something different. Something more special about being here with Emily. When he opened the hymnal and his voice rose up with hers on the opening carol, something stirred in his heart that had been quiet since he was a child.

Poinsettias decorated the altar with a manger scene standing to one side. Slade became increasingly aware of the sense of community here, of everyone knowing everyone else, and caring that they were all together on this night. There was scripture reading and prayers for those who were sick, rejoicing for those who had gotten married and babies who were born. And then there was the sermon. During it, Emily's hands lay in her lap, her shoulder companionably brushing Slade's. She turned to look at him once, and their eyes locked for a few long moments.

He leaned close to her and murmured in her ear, "I'm glad you invited me along tonight."

She just smiled, and he wondered where her thoughts were, if she was remembering other Christmases, maybe with her husband. He didn't have a clear picture of Pete Lawrence and knew that could only come from her when she was ready to tell him about her marriage.

After the blessing and the final hymn, the minister stood in the small vestibule greeting the members of his congregation.

But before they reached the man, Dallas tapped Emily on the shoulder.

As soon as Dallas O'Neill's arm went around Emily's shoulders, she saw the expression on Slade's face. *He really is jealous of Dallas,* she thought, and realized it gave her an odd sense of satisfaction. When she'd seen Slade tonight in his Western-cut jacket, his string tie and his white shirt, a lightning thrill had run through her. He had a rugged face, but to her he was the most handsome man she'd ever seen. Everything about him tonight seemed larger than life, and she realized her attraction to him was becoming stronger, not lessening. Even while they sat in church listening to the sermon, it had been so strong she'd wanted to take his hand, feel his strength around hers. The feeling had been over-whelming.

So overwhelming that now she hugged Dallas gratefully, glad for the familiar, thankful that he had always been a steady friend in an uncertain world. "Merry Christmas, Dallas," she said as she leaned away from the hug.

"Merry Christmas to you, too." Dallas nodded to Slade. "Coleburn."

"Merry Christmas, O'Neill," Slade said tersely, with not a lot of enthusiasm behind it.

Dallas addressed Emily. "Mom said she was go-ing to invite you to Christmas dinner tomorrow. Are you coming?"

Emily had forgotten all about the invitation in her distinct awareness of Slade. "I haven't discussed it with Slade yet. I told her I'd give her my answer when we returned from church tonight."

"Well, I hope you come. Are you going to the Diamonds' New Year's Eve party?"

Turning to Slade, Emily included him in the con-versation. "One of the ranchers, Amos Diamond, raises quarter horses. Every New Year's Eve he has a party in his training arena. People come from miles around."

"It sounds like a nice celebration," Slade re-marked flatly.

After a few more minutes of conversation, Dallas kissed Emily on the cheek and said good-night, then shook the minister's hand and left.

Slade was quiet as she spoke to the minister and introduced him. They left the church, and Slade's silence on the way to the van bothered Emily. Con-cerned, she clasped his arm. "What's wrong?"

Standing in the glare of the floodlight that lit the parking lot, Slade's Stetson shaded his face. "If you want to go to dinner at the O'Neills tomorrow, feel free."

She knew how many Christmases Slade had spent alone. She would never leave him alone this year, not just out of kindness but because she wanted to be with him. "You're invited, too."

"I'm an afterthought."

"That's not true, and I won't go unless you come with me. I don't want to spend Christmas without you."

"You're a good-hearted woman, Emily, but I don't want your pity."

"Do you see pity?" she asked as she looked up at him.

When he didn't answer, she released his arm. "We can do whatever you'd like, Slade. I can make dinner or we can go to the O'Neills. It doesn't matter to me either way."

Some of the rigidity went out of his stance. "I'll tell you what. I'll go with you to the O'Neills tomorrow if you go with me to that New Year's Eve party and we call it a real date."

She thought about Slade moving on, she thought about his conversation with his brother and what that would mean to his life. "You'll be staying after Christmas?"

"I've given it some thought. Mark asked me to go with him to his Fun Festival next week. You still need someone to handle the chores. It's probably better if I just stay put until Hunter gets back to the country. Then I'll work out what comes next."

Her heart rejoiced that he wasn't leaving yet, but

her common sense told her not to be too happy about it. Still the idea of a real date was thoroughly exciting. "I'd like to go with you to the Diamonds' party."

He tilted his head and the play of light shone in his eyes. Or maybe the sparks there had nothing to do with the light. Maybe they came from the desire that she felt acutely, too.

"It's a date, then," he said, his voice deep and husky.

A night alone with Slade. She realized their relationship had just moved to another level. That idea made her all quivery inside, and she didn't know if the feeling was from anticipation or fear.

On the ride home, Slade switched on the radio and the soft strains of Christmas carols filled the inside of the van. Slade let Emily out at the door when he reached her house. She was accepting Mavis' invitation to Christmas dinner as he came inside.

Mavis gave Emily a hug. "We're glad you're going to join us tomorrow." Then she shook Slade's hand. "Merry Christmas, Slade. I hope you like ham because that's what we're having this year."

"Ham's just fine, ma'am."

As Emily hung up her coat, Slade walked Mavis to her car and made sure she was safely on her way.

"I know it's late," he said when he'd returned to the kitchen. "But I have something for you, and I'd like to give it to you tonight."

"Slade, you didn't have to—"

"It's Christmas, Emily. Just have a seat on the sofa. I'll be right there."

But instead of doing as he suggested, Emily went

to the tree and beneath it found a package she'd wrapped. She sat on the sofa, nervously made sure the baby monitor was adjusted properly and was laying the present on the coffee table when Slade came back into the room. He'd taken off his jacket and his shoulders seemed even broader in the white shirt. His hair fell rakishly over his brow, and his crooked smile made him look like a boy on Christmas.

He handed her a present wrapped in red paper and tied with a gold bow. "Go ahead," he said, sitting down beside her. "Open it."

After she untied the bow, she ripped off the paper and found a shoe box.

He grinned at her. "It was the only one I could find."

When she lifted the lid, she found tissue paper. Pushing it back, she didn't know what to expect. Inside lay a carved fawn, and she took it out reverently. "Slade, this is beautiful." And then she guessed. "Did you do this?"

"I've been carving since I was a boy. In my spare time. It keeps me out of trouble."

Examining it more closely, she turned the fawn in her hand and tears came to her eyes. "Thank you. It's the most beautiful present I've ever received." Without thinking, she leaned forward and kissed his cheek. It was a different kind of kiss than the others they'd shared, but in its way, it was just as special. She could see that Slade thought so, too, when she looked into his eyes. Taking a deep breath, she lifted her package from the table and laid it on his lap.

Slade made quick work of the wrappings then lifted the lid of the flat box. He saw the socks first and held them in his hand. "These will be great for working out in the barn. They'll keep me warm." Then he noticed the book. It was small, and as he lifted it out, he saw that it was a guide to the heavens.

"I didn't know if you still had the other one," she said softly.

"I don't. One of the bunkhouses I stayed in leaked with the rain and it got ruined a few years ago." Looking down at her, he said, "Thank you. Maybe you and I could go stargazing some night."

There was a mesmerizing quality about Slade's blue eyes that kept her from looking away, that kept her from wanting to hide, that kept her right where she was. Taking the deer from her hands, he set it on the coffee table and then his presents, too. There was a masterfulness about his movements and a surety. The same was true of his lips when they came down on hers, and she leaned into his kiss. He pulled back once, studied her face, and then kissed her again with demand, hunger, and the desire that had been building between them from the moment they'd met. Emily was totally lost in the sensuality of his lips and his tongue and his scent when she heard sounds coming from beside her.

Pulling away from him, she shakily ran a hand through her hair. "It's Amanda. I have to go to her."

Slade nodded. But as she picked up the fawn and went to the stairs, his gaze followed her. Finally he said, "One of these nights, Emily, nothing's going to interrupt us."

All the breath went out of her lungs and the force of what she felt for Slade made her put her hand on the banister for support. Then with a murmured "good-night," and "I'll see you in the morning," she mounted the stairs, needing the refuge of her bedroom.

She'd fallen in love with Slade Coleburn. What would she do when he left?

Chapter Eight

Big, fat flurries of snow blew around Emily and Slade as they entered the training arena where the Diamonds' New Year's Eve party was being held. Christmas had surpassed Slade's expectations for the day, beginning with Mark's look of glee as he saw his presents, his exclamations of delight as he opened each one. Emily had thanked Slade again for the fawn, and he'd felt pleased that she was keeping it near her in her room. Maybe it meant something to her. Maybe *he* was beginning to mean something to her.

That thought startled him. Did he want to mean something to her? He didn't know how to settle in one place. He didn't know how to be a husband or a father or the type of man a woman could need for longer than it took him to get restless and move on. The thing was—he'd had no sign of restlessness since arriving at the Double Blaze. He put aside that consideration to ponder later.

Slade wondered if Dallas O'Neill would be here tonight. He expected he would. Christmas Day would have been perfect if he hadn't been around. But Slade had managed to make polite conversation with him and act friendly for Emily's sake.

The inside of the arena was a sight to behold. Tables and chairs lined the perimeter. Bales of hay were stacked here and there for sitting, for leaning, and just for atmosphere, Slade supposed. At the far end, there was a stage, and a band was playing. A woman stepped up to the mike and began a familiar country tune. Evergreen boughs and red bows, intertwined with tinsel garlands, draped the walls.

"This is some shindig," Slade said close to Emily's ear.

When she turned to look up at him, her cheek almost brushed his. "Amos Diamond knows how to throw a party. He's not necessarily well-liked, but he *is* respected, and cutters come from all over the country to buy his quarter horses and have them trained."

A few coatracks filled the entryway to the arena. "Would you like to shed your coat?" Slade asked. "Or do you want to take it with you?"

"I can leave it here, then it won't be in the way." Holding it for her as she took it off, Slade's fingers brushed her shoulders and their gazes met. It had been that way since Christmas—the electric charge that ran through him whenever they touched, the tingling awareness of just being around her. He hung his own jacket beside her coat. He'd worn the white shirt and string tie along with the black jeans, and the way she was looking at him, he was glad he had.

"You look pretty tonight," he said simply, liking

the way she'd fixed part of her hair in a barrette in
the back, pulling it away from her face. She'd worn
lipstick again, too. Her long-sleeved red blouse had
a ruffle around the collar and around both cuffs.
Tiny blue embroidery decorated the placket. Her
blue denim skirt was full and had a ruffle around
the bottom that almost touched the instep of her
boots.

"Thank you," she murmured, blushing with his
compliment.

"You're welcome," he said with a smile, then
rested his hand at the small of her back and guided
her into the party. She didn't move away from him,
and he could feel the heat of her skin under the
cotton blouse. His fingers tingled, and his body
knew desire that was aching to be satisfied. Yet he
knew it might not be. He knew Emily's values.

They found seats at a table with people Emily told
him she had a nodding acquaintance with. Unlike
the women in the social hall after Thanksgiving,
these neighbors didn't seem curious about his relationship with Emily. They just wanted to have a
New Year's Eve to remember and that was fine with
him. Soon squares formed in the middle of the arena
and a caller came to the mike.

"Do you square dance?" Slade asked Emily.

"Since I was a kid," she answered with a smile.

Standing, he offered her his hand. She took it and
they joined one of the squares.

During the next hour, Slade glimpsed a side of
Emily he wished he knew better as she do-si-doed
and kicked up her heels with the best of them. She
was almost carefree while she laughed and talked
and joked with those around her as if she didn't have

a responsibility in the world. In his estimation, she had too many responsibilities, and he was glad that for this one night she could have some good old-fashioned fun. He'd like to see to it that she had more. He'd like to see to a lot of things.

When the squares broke up, they went back to the table for snacks and a drink, but then the band started playing a slow Kevin Sharp ballad, and Slade longed to hold Emily in his arms.

"Do you slow dance as good as you square dance?" he asked.

"I guess you'll have to dance with me to find out," she bantered back with an almost flirtatious look.

She was irresistibly pretty, sexy and sweet, and he led her out to the middle of the floor and took her into his arms. They'd touched and passed and connected now and then while they'd square danced, but this was altogether different. Holding her close, he brought her hand into his chest where he was sure she could feel the beat of his heart. The scent of her perfume was more intoxicating than years-old whiskey, and the ache inside him grew higher and wider and deeper. It was more than sexual and he didn't begin to understand it. It had to do with holidays and family and belonging in one place...to one person.

For how many years had he told himself he was a loner, and he liked it that way? But holding Emily in his arms, savoring the way she made him feel, told another story.

Her breasts pressed against his chest, and he ran his hand caressingly down her back. When she looked up at him, time seemed to stop. He bent his head, aware that her neighbors could be watching. Instead of kissing her, he brushed his cheek against hers, touched his lips to her temple and felt the softness of her hair across his jaw. It was more erotic than kissing in a way. More tantalizing. Bringing her even closer, he locked his hands at her waist and she linked her arms around his neck. They were swaying now rather than actually dancing. The closeness seemed necessary, part of who they were becoming... *what* they were becoming to each other. He was almost ready to forget about neighbors and gossip and kiss her right here in the middle of the party.

The music and voices and smells of hay and food and evergreen boughs seemed like a hazy reality to Emily as she danced with Slade. At that moment, he filled her world with power and strength and a protectiveness that felt oddly good. She'd never wanted to be protected, but with Slade, lots of things were different. A curling tension in her belly told her this man could arouse her to a height she'd never experienced. His looks, his slight touches, his scent, incited such a basic need in her that she'd been afraid of it. But tonight she was embracing it rather than fearing it. Tonight she wanted to explore it and, from the way Slade was holding her, she got the idea he wanted to explore it, too. When his lips grazed her temple, she drew in an unsteady breath.

But then suddenly, he put space between them.

When she looked up, she realized why. Dallas was standing there, looking serious and determined. "May I cut in?" he asked politely.

"That's up to Emily," Slade said tersely.

She didn't want to leave Slade's arms, but she

couldn't slight Dallas. Besides, she'd have the rest of the evening with Slade and a breather might do them both good. When she nodded and smiled at Dallas, Slade's arms slipped away from her, and she suddenly felt cold. One look at Slade's face told her she might have made the wrong decision.

But before he could turn away, she touched his hand. "Again later?"

His stormy blue eyes softened. "I'll be waiting," he said.

Dallas took her in a looser, less intimate hold.

"Are you getting serious about him?" Dallas asked without any preliminary conversation.

"I'm not sure what you mean by serious."

"Don't play word games with me, Emily. Are you losing your heart to him?"

She studied her longtime friend—the wayward lock of brown hair falling across his brow, his handsome face, his green eyes. "We've been friends a long time, Dallas. But I'm not comfortable discussing Slade with you."

"That about says it all." He gave her a probing look. "I guess it won't do any good if I warn you that you're going to get hurt."

"My eyes are wide-open and I know Slade will be moving on, if that's what you mean."

"I didn't think you were that kind of woman, Emily."

She stopped dancing. "What kind of woman?"

"Never mind," Dallas mumbled, looking unsettled.

"The kind of woman who sleeps with a man and then forgets about it?" she asked, angry now. "Seems to me, men find that idea just dandy. I don't see a ring on *your* finger yet. Are you going to tell me you've kept yourself for the right woman?"

Dallas's cheeks flushed and his green eyes flashed with gold, but then he let out a sigh. "Of course I'm not." He shook his head. "I should have remembered you can give as good as you get. Can we finish this dance or are you going to stand in the middle of the floor not moving?"

Wrinkling her nose at him, they took the traditional position again. "So when are you going to be home to stay?" she asked.

"At the end of August, I hope. But I'll be back and forth a few times before then. I've decided to build a house on the crest overlooking the north pasture. I'll be supervising basics from a distance, but then I'm going to do all the finish work when I get home."

"What type of house?" she asked.

He grinned as if just thinking about it made him happy. "A log home. Maybe you can help me decorate it."

"You don't want one of those big city ladies doing it?" she teased.

"You know what I think about city ladies, Emily."

The music stopped and she and Dallas separated. But he looked down at her fondly. "I wish you the best. You know that, don't you? I want you to be happy."

"I know you do. Thanks for caring about me, Dallas. It means a lot."

An emotion passed over his face that she didn't quite understand, but then it was gone and she thought maybe she'd imagined it because he smiled at her again. "Have fun with Slade tonight if that's what you want. And if I don't see you again later, I'll let you know when the ground breaking's going to be."

Emily stood on tiptoe and kissed him on the cheek. He moved away and waved before he headed for the front entrance. It looked as if he wasn't going to stay. She wished he'd find someone special.

Slade was involved in a conversation with the man beside him when she returned to their table. He ended it and stood. "Dallas left?" he asked with one arched brow.

"It looks like it."

"Good. Then I won't have to worry about anybody cutting in again. It sounds like another slow one. Are you ready?"

She was ready to be held in Slade's arms again and maybe she was ready for more.

As the saying went, they danced the night away, returning to the table now and then, but always eager to hold each other, sway to the music and sample pleasure that seemed forbidden in the midst of a crowd.

It was nearly midnight when Slade guided her away from the couples that were still dancing. Taking her hand, he led her behind a stack of hay bales.

"What's wrong?" she asked breathlessly as they finally stopped in a secluded corner.

"Nothing at all's wrong. I just thought we could use a little privacy when midnight finally struck."

Strains of Auld Lang Syne floated from the stage and someone began a countdown. She didn't need a crystal ball to figure out what Slade had in mind. "I think privacy's a great idea."

Looking up at him, she anticipated his kiss, ready to enjoy it fully. But just as Slade took her into his arms, there was a shuffle, a giggle and then, "Oops, I guess someone else had the same idea we did." Emily pulled away from Slade and saw Sharon Conner, a girl she'd gone to school with, standing beside a tall man.

She tried to hide her embarrassment. "Hi, Sharon."

"We'll find another corner," the brunette said with a smile. As she and her date walked away, Emily heard her say, "Emily was married to Pete Lawrence. I hear the guy she's with is a drifter, but anybody's got to be better than Pete."

The lights blinked, horns blew and Emily felt as if the whole world knew her business. Why had she come here tonight with Slade, letting herself open to gossip? Why had she thought she could have a good time and it would be no one's business but hers and Slade's?

"Emily?" Slade was looking down at her, his blue eyes pinning her still.

"We'd better go," she said.

But he clasped her shoulders and wouldn't let her turn away. "What did that woman mean?"

"This isn't the place—"

In the cacophony of voices and noisemakers and the band finishing their song, Slade raised his voice. "I think it's time you tell me about your marriage. I can wait another hour or so if you want to dance some more but we're going to talk about it tonight."

This time there was no way she could evade Slade's questions. The determined set of his jaw told her that. Part of her rebelled against Slade's decisive intent, but another part of her knew it was time to tell him. "I don't feel like dancing anymore. Let's go home."

Wind whistled against the cab of his truck as Slade drove back to the Double Blaze. He had a ton of questions. The cold penetrated the interior of the vehicle, though the heater strove to keep it warm. Emily sat close to her door as if she needed space between them, as if she were miles away. He decided to wait to begin until they got back to the Double Blaze.

Because of the cold wind, he let Emily out at the door by Rod and Mavis's utility vehicle. The couple had offered to baby-sit, saying they could have their own New Year's celebration in front of the TV.

After Slade parked the truck and went inside, he heard Mavis telling Emily, "Amanda just fell asleep. We let Mark stay up until ten and play cards with us. I hope that was all right."

Emily assured them that was fine, then took a loaf of cranberry bread she'd baked from the bread box and gave it to Mavis. Finally after hugs, handshakes, "Happy New Years" and the closing of the door, Slade and Emily were alone.

Slipping off his string tie, he laid it on the table and opened the top two buttons of his shirt. "I guess you want to check on the kids."

She nodded.

"I'll come up with you and say good-night to Mark if he wakes up."

Emily went up the stairs ahead of him and went to her bedroom while he pushed open Mark's door. The little boy was fast asleep, but he had kicked off his covers. Crossing the room, Slade pulled them up to Mark's neck and gave them a gentle pat. If he was a father, he could do this every night and never get tired of it.

But he didn't know how to be a father. No one had ever taught him. And to be a father, you had to stay in one place for a very long time.

Closing Mark's door, he saw the door to Emily's room was open. She was standing over Amanda's crib, looking down at her daughter. He stood beside her, aware of his heartbeat, aware of the rise and fall of Emily's breasts, aware of the little baby in the crib. The night-light by the dresser glowed dimly in the dark room.

"She's such a miracle, isn't she, Slade? When I hold her, when I feed her, sometimes I can't believe it." Emily looked up at him. "And you helped bring her into the world."

That was probably one of the proudest moments of his life, helping Emily bring a new life into the world. But looking down at Amanda, he realized she was the result of the union between Emily and Pete Lawrence and he couldn't wait a moment longer to ask the many questions that were stomping around in his head.

"Do you still love your husband?"

Emily's eyes widened and she looked surprised by the question. "No, I don't still love Pete. By the time he died...my feelings for him were almost gone."

Slade figured it would be better to start at the beginning. "How did you two meet?"

Stepping away from the crib, Emily sat on the corner of the bed. "In school. He was two years ahead of me. When he graduated, he got a job at a feed store in Billings. He started to come calling before I was out of school and, after I graduated, we got married. I just never realized..."

When she didn't continue, he prompted, "What?"

"Pete wasn't the man I thought he was. There was nothing terrible about our marriage. I guess some wouldn't even think anything was wrong with it. But Pete...I guess he just never wanted the responsibilities of being a husband or father. After we got married, we moved in here with Dad. Right away I started to see that Pete wasn't going to pull his share of the load. Dad never said much, but I know he minded for me. Pete wanted me to take care of him. Everything from his laundry to—" She stopped abruptly.

"Sex?" Slade asked pointedly and sat down beside her.

Her cheeks became red. "I don't want to go into that." After a pause, she went on. "I thought having a baby might make a difference. But after Mark was born, nothing changed except I had more to do. I tried to keep Pete happy. I tried to give him everything he needed, but it got to the point that I didn't know *what* he needed. He hardly talked to me...watched TV when he wasn't somewhere else. It was as if I was here for him, but he was never here for me. The year before he died, he took to drinking more. That's why his car went off the road."

There were a lot of things Slade wanted to say, but he knew he'd better not. He didn't want to offend Emily or her sense of propriety or her commitment to a marriage that obviously didn't have much good in it for her. But he did ask, "Why didn't you divorce him?"

"I believed in our vows. I believed if I kept trying hard enough..." She shook her head. "Amanda was an accident. I didn't even know I was pregnant until after Pete died."

"I don't know much about marriage," Slade said gruffly. "But I suspect just one person can't make it work." There was something else he had to ask. "Was Pete ever...rough with you?"

Her reply was instantaneous. "Oh, no, never. It's just...the feelings I had for him changed so. I lost respect for him. After the first year of marriage, I realized I'd been infatuated with him. I wanted the security of being part of a couple, like other girls, and I thought him being older and all would give me that. But I wonder now if I was ever really in love with him. I'm determined never to want that again, to stand on my own two feet and make my own life."

After a long silence, Slade asked, "He wasn't much of a father to Mark, either, was he?"

She shook her head. "You've given him more time and attention since you've been here than Pete ever did."

The way she was looking at him made Slade's heart race so fast he could hardly breathe. He moved closer to her, and when she didn't inch away, he put his arm around her. "We haven't rung in the new year yet. Do you still feel like it?"

Her voice was almost a whisper, but he heard the soft "Yes."

When he took her lips, he couldn't get enough. At the party, he'd intended to coax her, go slowly, deepen whatever bonds were forming between them. But now he couldn't even find slow, and they zoomed along to hot and hungry and passionate. The shadows of the room, the silence of night, the wind blowing against the windows invited intimacy. One kiss became two, and then another that seemed to last a lifetime. He stroked her hair and without knowing exactly how it happened, he found himself lying beside her on the bed, caressing her cheek, rasping his tongue against hers until time and place and reality slipped away. She was sweeter than any honey, her skin softer than any flower petal, her perfume so taunting it made him dizzy. Or was it the desire that was making his head spin and his body ache?

He couldn't help but want more, and his hand slid to the buttons on her blouse. He began unfastening them, one by one. She tugged his shirt from his jeans and when her hands splayed across his rib cage, he sucked in a breath and thought he'd die from the sheer pleasure of her touch. Her fingers sifted through his chest hair as he kissed her neck.

But when his hand came to her breast, she stopped him. "Slade, I can't." Jerking away, she sat up. "I mean I'm breast-feeding and—"

"I know you're breast-feeding, Emily. That's not news to me. Are you telling me I need to be careful? Are you saying—"

"I'm saying I can't do this."

"What can't you do, Emily?"

"I thought I could just be here with you. I thought I could let you kiss me and touch me, but…"

"Is it too soon?" He was still looking for a sane reason for her stopping.

"No. But, Slade, that's not it. Even if we could, if we did, everything would change. I'd change. I'm not a woman who can lie with a man and forget about it in the morning. Don't you understand that?"

Oh, he understood it, and he wished to heaven he could change it. But he knew he couldn't. Emily was who she was. "Then what was tonight about?"

"I thought I could be different. I'm sorry. I should have known myself better."

Sitting up, he threw his legs over the side of the bed. "You don't have anything to apologize for. Neither of us does. This has been building ever since I arrived here, and maybe it's time I think about leaving. I told Mark I'd stay for his Fun Festival and I will. But I'll plan on heading out at the end of January."

She was silent for a few moments and then as she buttoned her blouse, she said, "If you think that's best."

Pushing himself to his feet, he looked down at her. "I do. For all of us. But I think it will be better if we don't tell Mark just yet. Let's wait till closer to the time."

"If that's what you want," she said again in that polite tone, and he wished she'd say more. Yet he wasn't sure exactly what he wanted to hear.

At the door to her room, he stopped a moment and looked over at the crib, then he closed the door to Emily's bedroom and went downstairs thinking the new year was off to a hell of a start.

En route to Denver, Hunter Coleburn couldn't wait to land and call the brother he was determined to get to know. A week into the new year, after glancing out the window of the business jet into the dark night, Hunter turned his attention back to the papers in his hand. He'd wrapped up negotiations sooner than he'd expected, and he could have waited until morning to fly back to Denver. But once he'd landed in New York, his client had offered the use of his jet and Hunter had his reasons for wanting to return sooner rather than later. Though his gaze rested on the terms of a contract he was drawing up, his thoughts settled on Slade Coleburn.

He'd been stunned to learn he had a twin brother.

It was probably the second most important event in his life. The first…

He smothered thoughts of Eve Ruskin as he had for the past five years and focused rather on a childhood in a family where he'd never felt as if he quite belonged. John and Martha Morgan had given him tender care and a home as they had their two natural children. But Hunter had always felt different from his brother Larry and sister Jolene. Larry had always reminded Hunter he was adopted. And the light in John Morgan's eyes didn't seem to shine as proudly for Hunter as it did for his siblings. It was a gut-level feeling of aloneness that had been with him as far back as he could remember, and now maybe he knew the reason why.

When his father and mother had called him in London before Christmas, he'd finally learned the secret they'd been keeping.

Their conversation was etched indelibly in his mind.

"Hunter, your mother and I have something to tell you. She's on the other phone," John Morgan had said.

Hunter's stomach had clenched. Was one of them sick? Had something happened to Larry or Jolene? But before he could ask, his mother had admitted, *"Hunter. We've kept something from you all these years. We thought it was best, but..."*

"What is it, Mom?"

"You have a twin," his father answered.

Hunter had been stunned as he repeated, *"A twin?"*

"His name is Slade," John Morgan continued. There was a pause. *"This is complicated to try to explain over the phone. But he's been searching for you. He put an ad in the paper, and I wrote to him. We received a picture from him and...you look alike. Slade's hair is brown and yours is black, but that's the only difference."*

Absorbing the idea that he had a brother he'd never known about took a few moments. *"Why didn't you ever tell me?"*

"We didn't know if he was still alive," his father responded gruffly. *"We were supposed to adopt both of you. But then a lot of things happened at once. Slade contracted pneumonia and was hospitalized. He wasn't responding to treatment. Your mother found out she was pregnant, and I was offered a job in Montana. We had to make decisions, Hunter, that were best for all of us. The boys' home wouldn't let us go through with Slade's adoption with him so sick. They said if he made it, they'd find a good family for him. With a new baby on the way,*

and moving, our budget was already stretched tight...''

''So you left Slade behind.''

''Yes.''

Hunter had taken a deep breath. ''Do you have a number where I can reach him?''

''Yes.'' *His father gave it to him, then added,* ''He's at the Double Blaze Ranch near Billings.''

''Hunter?'' *his mother had asked softly.*

''Yes, Mom.''

''We'll talk about all of this when you get back.''

Now he was coming back. What was there to discuss? They'd left his twin behind, and Hunter didn't know if he could ever forgive them for that.

Hunter wasn't the type of man to believe in psychic connections. He didn't believe in what he couldn't see, touch, or feel. Yet as soon as he'd heard Slade's voice... Maybe meeting Slade could affect the well of emptiness inside him, as meeting Eve had so many years ago.

Eve. Usually she only disturbed his dreams, not his waking moments.

Again pushing thoughts of her into a closed box in his mind, he thought about meeting his brother face-to-face.

The pilot announced that it was snowing in Denver but the airport was open. They would be landing in ten minutes. Hunter gathered the papers on his lap. He'd been too distracted to work. That wasn't like him. With a frown, he stuffed papers into a folder, then into his briefcase. Rolling down his white shirtsleeves, he fastened the buttons on the cuffs, eager to land, eager to make a call to his brother. In his eagerness, he forgot to fasten his seat belt and instead planned a trip to Montana in his mind and determined how long he could stay. A week, maybe ten days. He had an important merger meeting on the twentieth.

Hunter hardly even noticed the descent of the plane. But suddenly it was hitting the runway hard. The jolt threw him out of his seat and, as the plane skidded crazily and crashed into something with a crunch of metal, his head hit the floor, and everything went black.

Chapter Nine

As Emily sorted the stack of clean laundry on the kitchen table, she picked up a pair of Slade's underwear. Quickly folding it, she couldn't help remembering New Year's Eve, their interlude on her bed and the distance that had been between them ever since. Her heart ached when she thought about him leaving. That night, she'd realized she loved him enough to make love with him, to spend the rest of her life with him. But he wasn't the type of man to commit himself to marriage, and she couldn't settle for less.

It was nearly suppertime when the kitchen door flew open, then slammed as Mark bounded in. He'd been tending the animals with Slade in the barn. He was always running or slamming, but that was the way boys were and no amount of scolding would change it. Only age might. "Slade says we're gonna win on Friday. Think we can, Mom?"

The day after tomorrow was Fun Festival Day at

school. Mark was so excited about the day, he'd been talking about it for the past week.

The kitchen door opened again, and Slade came inside. As he hung up his hat and coat, she said to her son, "I think the important thing isn't winning but having fun."

"Your mom's right, Mark. It doesn't matter if we win or not." He reached over and rumpled Mark's hair. "But winning would be nice, too. And if we do our best, there's no reason why we can't take that prize."

When the phone rang, Slade reached for it.

Emily knew he was expecting a call from his brother. He'd been restless the past few days, hardly ever still, and Emily suspected he'd be gone *before* month's end.

Slade greeted the caller, but when he didn't speak for a long while, Emily glanced at him and saw something was terribly wrong. Mark was still chattering, and she handed him a pile of Slade's clothes, asking the boy to take them to his room.

"I understand," Slade said into the receiver. "I'll get there sometime tomorrow." After a few more moments of silence, he responded, "Don't worry about that. I'll rent a car and come straight to the hospital. If he— Never mind. Just hold on, Mr. Morgan. We'll start praying at this end, too."

As Slade hung up, Mark returned to the kitchen.

Slade's expression was grim, and he motioned Mark to a kitchen chair. "Sit down, partner. I have something to tell you. You know that brother I told you I was going to meet soon?" At Mark's nod, he went on. "He was in an accident yesterday, and he's not doing too well. He hasn't regained consciousness and the doctors are afraid…'' Slade cleared his throat. "I have to fly to Denver as soon as I can.''

"But you'll be back Friday?'' Mark asked.

The expression on Slade's face made Emily ache for him. "No, I won't be back for Friday. I know this is a disappointment to you, and I promise when I get back I'll make it up to you somehow.''

Crossing to her son, Emily put her arm around his shoulders. "Mark, this isn't something Slade can help. You have to try to understand.''

"I *don't* understand. You said you were going to be there and now you're not.'' He tore away from Emily and ran up the stairs.

Slade ran his hand down over his face. "I know I'm letting him down, but I can't wait till Saturday to leave. Hunter came home yesterday in somebody's corporate jet. With the snow, something happened on the landing and the plane crashed into a truck. Hunter's leg is broken. They took care of that, but he hasn't regained consciousness and they don't know if he will. His dad was pretty upset.''

"Mark will get over this,'' she said, not really sure he would.

"Will he? And are you going to be able to manage while I'm gone?'' Slade swore. "I feel as if I'm deserting you.''

"You were going to leave at the end of the month anyway.''

That simple truth hung between them. Once Slade left for Denver, she didn't think he'd ever return. Men like him moved on and didn't look back.

"I've got to call the airline,'' he said gruffly, pushing back his chair and going to the phone. "I'll probably have to wait till morning to get a flight out.'' Pulling out the nearest drawer, he found the phone book and laid it on the counter with a thump.

Emily's heart felt as if it were breaking in two. She loved this man. She didn't want him to leave the Double Blaze or her life. But she knew there was nothing she could do about it if he did.

Slade tried to talk to Mark that night and again early the following morning, but the seven-year-old didn't understand why he had to leave. He only knew the man he'd looked up to was breaking his promise.

Slade's goodbye to Emily was brief. He hadn't touched her or kissed her since New Year's Eve because he thought that was the way she wanted it. But leaving her now was harder than he ever imagined it could be. He told her he'd call as soon as he knew when he was coming back, but there was a look in her eyes that made his gut clench. It was sorrowful and yearning, yet resigned, too. He'd packed everything, telling himself he didn't know how long he'd be in Colorado.

When he drove away, he glanced in his rearview mirror, and saw Emily standing on the porch gazing after him. On the flight to Denver, Slade felt as if he'd left a piece of himself back at the Double Blaze, but then his thoughts centered on Hunter and what he might find when he reached the hospital.

It was late afternoon when Slade rented a car, drove to the hospital and found Hunter's room. A lump clogged his throat as he stood in the doorway. A distinguished brown-haired gentleman with a receding hairline sat on one side of Hunter's bed. His shirt and slacks were a bit rumpled, and Slade wondered if he'd spent the night at the hospital. On the other side of the bed, an ash-blond-haired woman with more gray than blond shining in her short curls kept vigil, holding Hunter's hand. Then Slade's gaze rested on the man in the bed. His leg was in a cast and elevated. There were bruises along one side of his face, and an oxygen tube rested at his nose. He appeared to be sleeping. Except for his black hair, Slade could have been looking into a mirror.

There was a soft gasp, and Slade realized the woman had seen him.

"Oh my, you *do* look alike." She rose from her chair and came immediately to Slade.

Taking off his hat, he extended his hand to her. "Slade Coleburn, ma'am."

Instead of shaking his hand, she clasped it with both of hers. "I'm Martha Morgan. We're so glad you could come."

Her husband stood and crossed to him, too. "Nothing's changed. Hunter's stable, but the doctors don't know if or when he'll wake up." Glancing over at his son, John Morgan's face showed all of his concern. "Our daughter went home to change clothes and get something to eat. And Larry—he's not coming in until tonight." John put his arm around his wife, glanced at Hunter, then back at Slade. "We'll go get some coffee."

The Morgans were going to leave him alone with his brother, and Slade was grateful for that. This wasn't the way he intended their meeting. This wasn't what he'd expected at all. After he forced a smile for the Morgans' benefit and they walked down the hall, Slade came deeper into the room and stopped at the foot of the bed. His twin brother. He took the chair that John had left and sat down to keep his own vigil. He couldn't seem to find any words. He couldn't seem to say all the things he'd been thinking.

All he could do was lay his hand on Hunter's arm and murmur, "I'm here, Hunter."

Later that evening Slade met Hunter's siblings. Like Hunter's parents, Jolene greeted him warmly. She had her father's dark brown hair. Larry Morgan, on the other hand, shook hands with Slade but seemed remote. Blond like his mother, he didn't have her outgoing personality and kept his distance. Slade figured he was worried like they all were. All in all, the Morgans were nice, the kind of family Slade had always dreamed of having. Would Hunter even want Slade in his life when he already had so much family?

On Friday afternoon, Slade sat by Hunter's side again, while the Morgans took a break. John and Martha had insisted he stay at their house last night instead of at a hotel. He'd refused at first, but when they'd looked so upset at his refusal, he'd given in. Pulling him aside at one point, Jolene had told him that her mother needed someone to take care of. Since she couldn't do anything for Hunter, Slade's staying at the house would help her cope. So Slade had let Mrs. Morgan whip up an omelet for him after he'd taken her home while he told her something about the life he'd led. John had remained at the hospital throughout the night, coming home in the early morning to catch a few hours of sleep while Jolene sat with Hunter. After lunch Slade drove the Morgans back to the hospital.

Around two John and Martha took a walk, giving

Slade time alone with Hunter. When he checked his watch, Slade realized Mark would be building a snowman about now. He still felt bad about leaving, but as Emily had said, he'd be doing it eventually.

He looked down at his brother, willing him to live, willing him to be healthy again. And suddenly he understood that maybe willing it wasn't enough. Maybe he had to come right out and say it. Maybe he had to introduce himself to this person who had shared a womb with him.

"Hunter, I know your mom and dad have been talking to you, but I kinda felt foolish about it. Maybe it's time I forget about feeling foolish. You're the brother I never knew, the family I never had. You can't slip away now that we found each other. Hunter, can you hear me?"

Watching closely, he examined his twin brother for any sign of acknowledgment, any sign that he wanted to come back to the world of the living. He thought he saw Hunter's eyelashes flicker. "Can you hear me, Hunter? Show me somehow that you can. Come back here so I can get to know you."

At first Hunter Coleburn didn't respond, but then a muscle under Slade's fingers jumped, and his brother's eyes fluttered open. They were intent on Slade, and Slade couldn't speak for the thankfulness filling his heart.

"It's good...to meet you...brother." Hunter's voice was gravelly and slow.

Slade wanted to shout for the Morgans and the nurse. Instead he just gripped Hunter's arm and pushed the call button, saying, "Don't you know better than to land when it's snowing?"

A grimace twisted Hunter's lips. "I wanted to get home…and call you. Is the pilot okay?"

Letting what Hunter had said settle in, Slade answered, "He's fine. Shaken up mostly. How are you feeling?"

"I have a hellish headache. And I'm thirsty."

Slade poured water from the bedside container into a glass and helped Hunter take a few swallows. Their gazes connected, and Slade felt a bond like he'd never known. "Your parents went for a walk. They'll be back soon."

Hunter lay back on the pillows again.

"I met your sister and brother last night," Slade added, giving Hunter time to orient himself.

But Hunter was alert. "What do you think of all of them?" His voice was coarse, but steady now.

Before Slade could answer, the nurse rushed in. When she saw Hunter was awake, she checked his vitals, nodded with a smile and said, "I'll page the doctor."

When she'd gone, Hunter and Slade gave each other the once-over again, and then they both smiled. "It's strange, isn't it?" Hunter noted.

"You mean facing yourself? Sure is. But I imagine we're more different than alike. We've lived different lives."

"Maybe."

There was a long silence.

"So…you were going to tell me what you think of my family," Hunter prompted.

"Your parents are great. Jolene made me feel welcome, too. I didn't spend much time with Larry."

Hunter closed his eyes for a moment, then after a pause, opened them once more and gazed at Slade.

"I always felt adopted. Because of that, I always felt...alone. I guess that's hard to understand."

"I understand feeling alone. I have all my life. But now seeing you—it's going to make a difference knowing you're here."

Hunter nodded while they absorbed it and then he asked, "Did Mom and Dad tell you what happened back then? Why we were separated?"

Slade shook his head.

Hunter looked pensive. "There will be time for that. They should tell you themselves. How long can you stay?"

As soon as Slade knew Hunter would really be all right, he had to get back to Emily and Mark. He had to. "Just a little while this time. I have to settle some things in Montana. But then I'll be back."

First he had to make sure Emily could manage without him.

The hospital bill for charges after Amanda's birth had come the day Slade left, and Emily had known then she was in trouble. It wasn't just the hospital bill. But that was the straw that caused her to take the real estate agent's card from her wallet and call him. He'd been eager to talk to her, and she'd gone into town to meet with him the same day.

Sunday afternoon, she sat at the table with receipts and bills from the past year spread around her. Pete had the Double Blaze mortgaged to the hilt, and she simply couldn't keep up. It wasn't merely the slipping further and further into more debt. She'd also been foolish to think she could care for the ranch on her own with two children. But she'd wanted to try. She'd grown up here and the thought of leaving...

Tears came to Emily's eyes, but she knew she couldn't be weak now. She had to be strong to make a future for her children. They'd move into Billings, and she'd get a job clerking in a store or typing. Maybe she could take one of those courses on computers. She'd do whatever she had to to make her children's lives secure.

When the phone rang, her heart leaped, and she told herself not to expect to hear Slade's voice when she picked up the receiver. Since Thursday after he'd left, she'd jumped every time the phone rang. But why would he call her if he wasn't coming back? And she believed he wasn't.

"Emily?" asked a deep baritone she instantly recognized.

"Hi, Slade." She tried to keep the emotion from her voice. She tried to pretend he was simply a stranger she'd hired to help with the chores.

"How are you?" he asked, concern in his tone.

She realized she didn't want his concern. She wanted his love for a lifetime. But she couldn't have that, so she answered, "We're fine."

After a pause, he asked, "Did Mark enjoy the Fun Festival?"

"He didn't go." She'd coaxed and coaxed, told him she'd call Rod O'Neill. But Mark had been adamant. If he couldn't go with Slade, he didn't want to go.

"He's still mad at me."

"I've explained over and over again about your brother, but Mark was just terribly disappointed. How is Hunter?"

"He's going to be fine."

There was relief in Slade's voice and something else, maybe almost a jubilance. If he wanted a connection, she supposed he'd found it. "That's terrific."

"Emily?"

"What?"

"Stop talking to me as if I'm not me and you're not you. I'll be back soon."

"You're coming back?"

"I told you I would."

If he was coming back, she had some things to tell him. "I'm putting the ranch on the market, and I'm moving to Billings."

"You're what? When did all this happen?"

"The hospital billed me, and I was going through last year's receipts for taxes. I can't stay here, Slade. I just can't. I have to build a life for Mark and Amanda, not try to hold on to the past."

Silence stretched between them until finally Slade said, "I'll be back tomorrow, and we'll talk about it."

"There's nothing to talk about."

"Oh, yes, there is. So don't do anything you'll regret until I get there. Understand?"

She'd already done something she regretted. She'd lost her heart to Slade Coleburn.

When the house came into sight, Slade stepped on the accelerator a little harder, knowing that wasn't a good thing to do on the snow-packed road. But he'd missed Emily and the ranch more than he could ever say. The thought of her selling the Double Blaze just tore at him, though he wasn't sure why.

The conversation he'd had with Hunter and his parents about what had happened over thirty-one years ago seemed distant now. Although Hunter hadn't said so, Slade could see his brother was bothered that the Morgans had left Slade behind back then. But as Slade had told Hunter later when they were alone, burned bridges were dangerous to cross. They'd found each other and that's what mattered now. Hunter had agreed, but Slade had seen pain in his brother's eyes that had nothing to do with his accident. It would take some time to learn about each other...to really get to know each other.

After Slade parked his truck, he grabbed his duffel bag and hurried to the house. As he opened the kitchen door, the scene greeting him sent a surge of longing through him—Mark was sitting at the table doing his homework and, as always, great smells filled the kitchen. Emily was stirring something on the stove and all he wanted to do was go to her, lift her into his arms, kiss her and hold her. But instead he stood there and absorbed her smile. She looked happy to see him.

"How was your flight?" she asked.

He dumped his duffel bag on the floor, placed his Stetson on the rack, then hung up his jacket. "Just fine. Hey, Mark, how are you doing?"

Mark laid down his pencil and mumbled, "I'm going up to my room."

But Emily frowned. "Slade greeted you, Mark. Don't be rude."

The boy looked at his mother and then at Slade.

"Hi, Slade." Then he asked, "Now can I go to my room?"

"Maybe you and I should have a talk first," Slade said soberly. "I hear you didn't go to the Fun Festival."

"I didn't want to."

Slade went over to Mark, pulled out a chair and sat facing him. "I'm sorry I couldn't be here for you, but you should have let your mom call Rod. You should have gone."

"Rod isn't…" He stumbled for a moment. "Rod isn't like a dad. All the other kids had their dads there."

Mark's words were like a punch in Slade's gut, and he realized how much he'd hurt this little boy that he'd come to be so fond of. "Would you let me make it up to you?"

"How?" Mark asked, looking interested.

"Let me think about it tonight, okay?"

Mark looked pensive for a moment, then nodded. "Okay."

Soft cries of Amanda waking came from the living room. Mark hopped up from his chair and ran, saying, "I'll tell her you're coming."

After Emily turned off the stove, she would have passed Slade, but he stood and caught her arm. "Let me give you the capital you need to keep this place running."

"You have no idea how much that would be."

"And you have no idea how much I have saved. I've worked since I was eighteen and hardly spent anything."

After a good long minute, she asked, "And why would you give it to me?"

"Because I don't need it and you do." He could have sworn she looked disappointed at his reason, but he didn't know why.

"I can't accept money from you, Slade. I have to make a life for me and Mark and Amanda on my own."

"If you won't take it as a gift, consider it a loan."

She vehemently shook her head. "The reason I'm doing this is because I'm tired of being in debt. Whether it's a gift or whether it's a loan, I'd be in your debt and that's not acceptable to me. But don't think I don't appreciate your offer, because I do."

Amanda's cries were still soft and nondemanding, more of a notice that she was awake rather than particularly hungry. So Slade kept his hand on Emily's arm, wanting to touch her less casually, more intimately. "Do you *want* to sell the Double Blaze?"

"No, I don't want to sell it! But there isn't another solution. I've already spoken to a real estate agent. I'm going into town to sign the papers tomorrow. It will go on the market next Monday."

"Why won't you accept my help?" He wanted to shake her and kiss her and satisfy his longing for her all at the same time.

"Because I've already accepted too much of your help, Slade. It's time we both moved on."

He knew she was right, and moving on was exactly what he'd planned. But it didn't sound right and it didn't feel right.

The cries from the living room became louder and more intense, and Emily pulled away from his clasp. Ever since New Year's Eve, he'd felt the determination in Emily to put him out of her life. And he knew why. She was the type of woman who needed a permanent commitment. He had never known permanency of any kind. He'd be a bad risk, and he knew Emily wasn't the type of woman to take risks. She was too protective of herself and especially of her children.

He might be going back to Denver to see Hunter sooner than he'd expected.

It wasn't just the Fun Festival that had been important to Mark, Slade knew. It was the atmosphere of it. The kids, the fun, the noise. So Slade decided to create that atmosphere again in a smaller way. After speaking with Emily and the parents of a few of Mark's friends, he planned an afternoon at the ranch of games, building a snow fort and snowball battles. Although the parents were invited, too, since they'd already taken time for one Fun Festival, they just dropped off their kids to enjoy the fun.

Slade joked and laughed and roughhoused with the boys as they built a wall of snow and then torpedoed snowballs at each other, running behind the wall, bumping into each other, laughing. He was glad the weather had cooperated, and they could stay outside for a bit. After they went into the house, Emily did her part by providing hot chocolate and cookies. They even toasted marshmallows in the potbellied stove. Afterward in the barn, Slade showed the boys some roping skills. Mark looked as if he was having fun, and when everyone said goodbye, Slade thought the afternoon had gone particularly well.

After the last boy left, Slade found Mark in his

room where he was putting on his sneakers. "Did you have fun this afternoon?" he asked him.

"Sure," Mark said, tying one shoe.

"I bet it was just as much fun as the Fun Festival," Slade remarked, hoping Mark would tell him it had been.

But Mark murmured, "The dads weren't here."

"I was here."

"Yeah, but you were playing with all of us. It just wasn't the same as...me pretending you were my dad for the day."

The word "pretending" bothered Slade, as did the rest of what Mark had said. But he had nothing to say to contradict him. All he could think of was, "Maybe someday you'll have a dad of your own."

After Mark tied his other shoe, he looked up. "I want you to be my dad."

Mark's declaration made Slade take a deep breath. "I don't know how to be a dad, Mark. I never had one myself. I haven't even spent time around kids and their dads. You need someone who's an expert at it."

The little boy's brown eyes were accusatory. "You could be a dad if you wanted to. I know you could. But I guess you don't want to."

"Your mom has a say in this," Slade said a tad defensively.

"You could convince her. I know you could."

Before Slade could find an adequate response, Emily called up the stairs. "Slade, telephone. It's your brother."

Slade said to Mark, "We'll talk more about this later," and went downstairs, concerned something was wrong in Denver.

But nothing was wrong. Hunter was just checking in after being released from the hospital, telling Slade how restless he was. The doctor hadn't wanted him to be alone, so instead of going to his penthouse, he was staying with his parents for a few days.

"Mom wants to wait on me hand and foot," he complained.

Slade laughed. "That's what mothers do, Hunter."

There was silence. "I guess that's true. I'll stop complaining and be thankful. It almost feels as if—" He cut off abruptly and changed the subject. "When can you come back to Denver?"

Slade glanced at Emily who was sitting in the living room with Amanda. "I'm not sure yet. I'll let you know in a few days."

After Slade hung up, he crossed to the living room and just stood watching Emily with her daughter. Apparently Amanda had finished eating and was cuddling against Emily's breast.

"Is everything okay?" Emily asked when she looked up and saw him watching her.

"Yeah. Hunter's home from the hospital. He must be feeling better. He can't wait to get back to his own place." Slade's talk with Mark had made him feel restless and even more guilty for leaving when he had. "I want to get Mark that bicycle."

"Why?"

"Because I feel I let him down by leaving. He had fun this afternoon, but he says it wasn't the same as the Fun Festival."

"And you think a bicycle will make up for you not going?"

She made it sound like some kind of bribe. "Hell, Emily, I don't know."

"Have you told Mark you're leaving?"

Leaving. The word had never bothered him before. Neither had the thought of moving on. "No, I haven't."

"I'm going to start packing up the attic tomorrow. The agent's bringing three people through on Monday. He doesn't think I'll have any trouble selling if we keep the price fair."

"I wish you'd reconsider my offer."

Her gaze was troubled as she shook her head. "I can't do that, Slade. I can't..." She cleared her throat and looked down at her baby. "I'm going to start a new life. That will be best."

The thought of Emily starting a new life made Slade's chest tighten. He wished... Knowing wishes didn't count much against reality, he mumbled, "I'm going to take care of the horses."

She didn't look up at him, and he imagined she didn't much care what he did.

Emily's sob escaped the same time the kitchen door closed, and she held her daughter and just rocked her. She didn't want Slade to leave; she didn't want to think about the rest of her life without him. But she couldn't put a fence around him. He'd offered her money to keep the ranch running. But she didn't want money.

She wanted him.

But she couldn't ask him to stay. He had a brother in Denver and miles to go before he settled down.

If he ever did.

Chapter Ten

The attic held a treasure full of memories. Emily tried to hold back tears the next day as she took advantage of Amanda's naptime to sort through years of her dad's possessions and her own. Finally she just sat in the middle of the attic on the floor and let the tears fall. She was crying because her dad would never meet his granddaughter. She was crying because she *did* love this house and the land and everything the ranch represented. She was crying because she loved Slade and wanted him to return that love, yet knew that he couldn't.

She had too much pride to ask him to stay. She had too much pride to accept his help. She had too much pride to love a man again who couldn't love her.

Slade was a kind, gentle, strong man who had so much to give. But his upbringing or lack of it had made him too restless to put down roots and, the irony was, he was searching for something he'd probably never find unless he *could* put down roots. But he had to come to terms with that on his own, and maybe he never would.

With a sigh, Emily rose to her feet and wiped the tears from her cheeks. She couldn't get anything done like this. Maybe if she started actually packing instead of just sorting she'd make some headway. She knew for certain she wanted to take along her dad's pipes. They still smelled liked the tobacco he'd used. She could remember him smoking while he told her stories. She'd also take along his arrow-head collection and some of the small antique tools he'd collected over the years. But she had to wrap it all carefully. She'd brought a few boxes to the attic but no newspaper.

As she went down the stairs into the room that would have been the nursery, Mark came running in. "Can I go out to the barn and help Slade?"

He'd been playing in his room and she guessed he was bored. "Tell you what. If you go out to the shed and get some newspapers for me, I'll make some hot chocolate. Then you can take it out to Slade."

Grinning, he nodded and raced down the stairs ahead of her to the living room. As he went to fetch his coat, she looked out the window. The sun was shining brightly, and the snow glittered with a sheen that was almost blinding. Icicles ran along the side of the barn's roof and the shed. Although the sun shone today, the weatherman was calling for a big snowfall again tomorrow. She hoped he was wrong. The sooner the real estate agent's clients could see the ranch, the sooner she'd sell it. It was going to hurt to let it go, so the quicker it was done, the better.

And the quicker Slade leaves, the better, her good sense told her. But she couldn't quite believe it.

As Mark put on his coat and boots, Emily took the cocoa from the cupboard.

He opened the door, called over his shoulder, "I'll be right back," and slammed the door shut.

As he scurried across the wooden porch, she shook her head.

While she took the milk from the refrigerator and set it to warm in a pan on the stove, she wondered what Amanda would be like at Mark's age, if she'd be a tomboy or like to wear dresses. Would Amanda miss having a dad as much as Mark seemed to? Slade would make such a good father if only…

Stop it, she scolded herself. You're only making it harder.

Emily's thoughts distracted her so thoroughly that the hot chocolate was finished before she realized Mark hadn't returned. Maybe he'd gone to Slade first to tell him he'd be bringing him the treat. Maybe he'd started helping Slade and forgotten about the newspapers. But he wouldn't forget the chocolate.

Crossing to the window, Emily looked outside, first at the corral, then at the shed. When her gaze fell on the small outbuilding, she gasped. Snow had mounded in front of the short door. If Mark had slammed the door when he went inside, the snow might have slid from the slanted roof and trapped him.

Acting on instinct, she grabbed her coat from a peg on the wall and kicked off her sneakers to slide into the boots on the mat by the door. Then she flew out the door, her coat flapping against her body as she ran across the gravel road to the shed, calling, "Mark? Mark?" She thought she heard crying as she neared the small building, and she called his name again.

"Mom," he shouted from inside. "I can't get out. Help me." At least five feet of snow had slid in front of the door. "Mom, I'm scared. It's dark in here."

"I know, honey. I'm going to get Slade."

"Don't leave me, Mom."

"Mark, listen to me. Take a deep breath and count to ten. You're going to be fine. I'll be right back."

She could still hear him crying and it broke her heart to leave him, but Slade could get him out faster than she could and they needed shovels. Slipping and sliding as she ran, she called Slade's name. When he came out of the barn, she yelled, "Get shovels. Mark's trapped in the shed. Hurry."

As she dashed back to the shed, Slade disappeared into the barn and soon came tearing after her. He brought two shovels and gave her the lighter, plastic one while he jabbed into the snow with the metal one he used for cleaning out the stalls. "Easy does it, Emily, it won't help Mark if you hurt yourself." His voice was gruff.

She knew he was thinking about her labor and having Amanda and still recovering from all of it, but apparently he also knew she couldn't stand by powerless. As they frantically shoveled the deep layers of snow, she called to Mark, "We'll have you out soon. Don't be scared, honey. We're right here."

"Slade, are you there?" Mark asked, tears in his voice.

"I'm here, son. Just hold on."

Snow flew as Slade practically burrowed it away, clearing twice as much as Emily at a time, forcefully pushing and throwing it until the door was clear. Then he opened the wooden door and Mark came tumbling out into his arms. Emily crouched down to hug her son, too, and the three of them held together for a few moments. When Slade's gaze locked to hers, she saw so much emotion there, her breath caught.

Maybe it was time to take a risk, to throw caution and pride to the wind....

Sucking in a deep breath, she put her own feelings aside for the moment and concentrated on her son, hugging him hard, letting him know he was safe. Finally she leaned back and took his face in her hands. "Are you okay?"

"It was so dark in there. I yelled and yelled, but I guess nobody heard me. And then I thought you might never find me—"

She hugged him close again. "I will *always* find you."

This time Mark pulled away and looked up at Slade. "I guess I shouldn't have cried."

Slade knelt down in the snow to look Mark straight in the eye. "There's nothing wrong with crying if there's a good reason for it, and you sure had one." Then Slade put his arms around Mark again, too, and Emily couldn't see his expression under the brim of his Stetson.

Slade's hands were shaking as he leaned away from the seven-year-old and got to his feet. His throat was tight, and his heart was beating so fast he didn't think it would ever slow down again. When Mark had rushed out of the shed into his and Emily's arms, Slade had glimpsed a vision of what life should be, could be, would be, if he had the courage to grasp it. Everything was suddenly so very clear to him. His feelings for Emily went much deeper than wanting to take her to bed—he needed her in his arms every day for the rest of his life. He needed to see her face when he woke up in the morning. He needed to kiss her when he came in from doing chores. He needed her warmth and determination and sweetness to give him direction and purpose and a reason to want to belong.

But he didn't know how to say any of that to her. Yet somehow he had to try. He had to tell her what was in his heart.

"I think we're going to have to heat up that hot chocolate all over again," Emily teased her son as she glanced at Slade. "Are you coming into the house?" she asked him softly.

He needed a few minutes to get his thoughts together. He needed to find the words that would convince her to spend her life with him. "As soon as I clean the rest of the snow from this roof. We don't want more falling."

Emily nodded, her eyes big and wide and...he wasn't sure what he saw there. Maybe it was just gratitude. But when she and Mark turned away and walked to the house, he knew she and the children had become his life.

When he let himself into the kitchen ten minutes later, Slade still didn't know what he was going to say or how he was going to say it. After he pulled off his boots and hung up his coat and hat, he saw that Mark was sitting on the sofa in the living room, a mug of hot chocolate in his hands, watching an animal show on TV.

Emily got up from the table and went to the pot on the stove. "Ready for that chocolate?"

"No."

His abrupt answer made her put the pot back down. "Would you rather have coffee?"

"Emily, I couldn't care less what I drink. I—" He stopped, feeling foolish and disconcerted and terrified as hell to tell her what was on his mind. But he was going forward and he wasn't looking back.

They spoke at the same time. His "I want you to marry me" got tangled up with her "I want you to stay."

"What?" they asked simultaneously.

Covering the distance between them swiftly, he clasped her shoulders. "Did you ask me to stay?"

She nodded. "Did you ask me to marry you?"

The uncertainty in her voice made him bring her closer into the circle of his arms. "I've got years of habits to break, Emily, and you're going to have to be patient with me. It's taken me a while to realize I want to do more than kiss you and find satisfaction with you under the covers at night. You've become part of me, and so have Mark and Amanda. Every time I thought about leaving, I got this sinking feeling in my gut, and I didn't understand what it was. Now, I do. I want to build a life here with you. I want to make you my wife. I want to be a dad to Mark and Amanda. I never knew what love was until I came here and found you. *Will* you marry me?"

There were tears in her eyes, but she looked up

at him with a smile that seemed to surround him. "Yes, I'll marry you. You're the finest, strongest, wisest man I've ever met. I love you, Slade Coleburn."

He couldn't believe his ears. He couldn't believe she felt the same. He couldn't believe she was going to be his. To make it all real, he took her into his arms and sealed his lips to hers. There was a depth to their kiss that hadn't been there before. All the barriers were down, and Emily responded with every bit of passion that he'd suspected was there. Their tongues danced against each other, their arms twined tighter, their bodies strained together until Slade knew he believed in dreams again and maybe even a heaven.

Absolutely absorbed in each other, Slade felt her start of surprise as if it was his own when he heard, "Wow! I never saw anybody kiss like that before."

Before he pulled away from Emily, he knew she was going to be flustered. He also knew becoming a father didn't start the day they got married. It started now.

He crooked his finger at Mark and when the boy came close, Slade laid a hand on his shoulder. "Remember when you said I could be your dad if I really wanted to?"

Mark's head bobbed up and down.

"Well, I really want to. How do you feel about me and your mom getting married?"

"You'll be my *real* dad and Amanda's, too?"

"I'd like to be. Since you're her big brother, and she can't talk yet, I guess you'll have to speak for both of you."

"I want you to be my dad, and so does Amanda," Mark added solemnly.

Slade curved his arm around Emily and his other around Mark. "Then let's set a wedding date."

Epilogue

Almost three weeks later, on Valentine's Day, Emily stood in the small dressing room off the vestibule of the church where she was about to get married, and tried to stand still as Mavis zipped up her wedding gown. It was cream satin, beaded at the sweetheart neck and down the long sleeves. Its full skirt made her feel like a princess.

"This is such a beautiful gown," Mavis said to her.

"It was all Hunter's doing. He has a client who designs wedding gowns. He sent me photographs and I picked one, and I can still hardly believe this is me." She'd curled her hair and arranged it on top of her head. The veil was simple, attached to a headpiece that slipped under her curls. The lace flowed down her back and she couldn't believe that in a few minutes, she'd be Slade's wife.

Slade's wife.

Tonight she would become truly one with him.

He'd insisted they not make love until their wedding night, knowing it would be more special that way. They weren't going on a honeymoon because of Amanda and Mark, but Slade had promised her that after they were all used to being a family for a while, the two of them could slip away for a weekend alone.

There was a loud knock on the dressing room door. "Who is it?" Mavis asked.

"It's Dallas. Can I come in?"

"Come on in," Emily called.

When he stepped into the room, he just stared at her for a few moments. "You look beautiful."

"Thank you," she murmured, glad Dallas could be here for this day.

"You'll be surrounded by well-wishers after the wedding," he concluded. "And I just wanted to tell you—" he paused for a moment "—that I hope you're always as happy as you look today. Last night I could tell that Slade's going to be the kind of husband you deserve."

Hunter had flown in yesterday, and last evening Emily had invited the O'Neills over to meet him. The tension that had once been there between Slade and Dallas had completely disappeared by the time the night was over. "I'm glad you can see that. He's going to be a terrific dad, too."

"It's obvious to anyone watching that you two are head over heels in love." He cleared his throat and went on, "His brother seems a decent sort. When I heard he was an international lawyer, I didn't think he'd fit in around here, but he's easy to talk to."

Emily had found Hunter more guarded than Slade, but friendly nonetheless. He seemed eager to get to know his brother, and that pleased her because she knew Slade wanted that, too. After the O'Neills had left last night, she'd found Hunter reading the wedding card Mavis had given her. He'd looked so sad. But when she'd asked him if something was wrong, the emotions had slipped from his face as if they'd never been there, and he'd said again how pleased he was that she and Slade had invited him to be part of their wedding. He considered it an honor to be Slade's best man.

Organ music began to filter into the dressing room. Dallas smiled. "I'd better find a seat." Then he kissed Emily on the cheek. "I promise I won't cut in when you and Slade are dancing at the reception."

After Dallas left the small room, Emily took a deep breath. "I guess it's time."

"It's time," Mavis agreed.

Rod was waiting in the vestibule. Emily had asked him to give her away. He'd been her dad's closest friend and it had seemed fitting. After Mavis handed Emily her bouquet of pink and white roses, the organist gave a cue and Mavis started down the aisle. Rod patted Emily's hand and said, "Here we go."

Emily began the walk up the aisle.

Only about ten of the church pews were filled with people. But Emily and Slade had decided to keep the ceremony small. Her friends were here, friends she hoped would become his friends. Grace Harrison and Mark stood in the front pew with Amanda, watching over her for Emily. Dallas was in the pew across from them where Rod would take his place as soon as he delivered her to Slade. When Emily looked up at the altar, she saw Hunter, his trouser leg slit over the cast that went from his foot to above his knee. He smiled at her, and she smiled back, feeling as if *she'd* found a brother, too.

But her gaze didn't rest on Hunter long. It moved to Slade, her husband-to-be. Walking toward him eagerly, she smiled up at him when Rod entrusted her to his care.

Slade leaned close to her and whispered in her ear, "I love you."

She took his hand. "I love you, too."

As they faced the minister, nothing had ever felt more right.

Completely aware of Slade and the binding words of the marriage ceremony, Emily's heart felt as if it would burst with happiness. Pictures of Slade's arrival at the Double Blaze, his help delivering Amanda, his tender words and passionate kisses, all played through her mind. When it came time for their vows, she turned to him and gazed into his eyes, longing to express everything in her heart. They'd decided to write their own promises to each other.

After Slade took both of her hands in his, she began, "I, Emily, take you, Slade, as my husband and partner and friend." She felt tears come to her eyes, but she kept going. "I promise to stand beside you no matter what life brings, to support you and listen to you, and to respect you every day of our lives. God sent you to me when I needed you most. You took care of me and Mark and Amanda as if we were precious to you. There are so many things about you that I love—your honesty, your strength, your gentleness."

Taking a deep breath, she ignored the tears rolling down her cheeks. "I vow to be faithful to you, to care for you and to trust you from this day forward as long as we both shall live."

The grip of Slade's hands told Emily that her words had touched him. He gazed down at her, his blue eyes tender and serious and loving. "Emily, I don't have fancy words for you. I just want to tell you what's in my heart. You are my home. I never had one of those. Growing up, dreams got lost in disappointment and in wanting to belong somewhere so badly, that I wasn't even sure what belonging meant. Because of you, I know."

His hands squeezed hers and he stopped for a moment as emotion welled up in his eyes. But he cleared his throat and went on. "You've become my sunshine, my peace, my reason to look toward the future. I love everything about you, from your sweetness to your stubbornness to your pioneer spirit. I pledge my love to you through good days, and bad days, and every other day in between. I promise to take care of you and protect you and to love Mark and Amanda as my own. And I vow to be faithful to you always. I love you, Emily, and I give you all that I am and all that I ever hope to be."

Gazing into each other's eyes, they absorbed the promises and their sacred commitment to each other, until Hunter tapped Slade on the shoulder and handed him a ring. Mavis gave one to Emily. Then they exchanged rings with the same fervor with which they'd exchanged vows. When the minister asked them to face forward for the final blessing, their hands were tightly entwined as were their hearts for all eternity.

At the end of the ceremony, the minister directed them to face the congregation. His voice rang out loud and clear. "I present to you, Mr. and Mrs. Slade Coleburn."

Applause rang out and Mark came racing over.

"Are you my dad now?" he asked.

Slade chuckled as Grace handed Amanda to Emily, and Slade put his arm around his new wife. "Yep. I'm your dad."

Mark grinned up at him. "Then we're a *real* family."

"A real family," Slade repeated.

Clapping his brother on the shoulder, Hunter grinned. "I think you forgot something. Isn't the groom supposed to kiss the bride?"

Emily knew Slade was being considerate of her in front of all these people, but she was proud of their union and needed to show him. She answered, "Yes, he is," and looked up at her new husband with all the passion and love she felt.

When Slade's lips touched hers, she kissed him fervently, looking forward to tonight with him, looking forward to all their days and nights. She'd found her life partner and her soul mate.

And she couldn't wait for their future to begin.

* * * * *

Be sure to look for the next book from Karen Rose Smith. Don't miss Hunter's story in JUST THE HUSBAND SHE CHOSE, *available in June from Silhouette Romance.*

If you enjoyed what you just read,
then we've got an offer you can't resist!

Take 2 bestselling love stories FREE!

Plus get a FREE surprise gift!

Clip this page and mail it to Silhouette Reader Service™

IN U.S.A.	**IN CANADA**
3010 Walden Ave.	P.O. Box 609
P.O. Box 1867	Fort Erie, Ontario
Buffalo, N.Y. 14240-1867	L2A 5X3

YES! Please send me 2 free Silhouette Romance® novels and my free surprise gift. Then send me 6 brand-new novels every month, which I will receive months before they're available in stores. In the U.S.A., bill me at the bargain price of $2.90 plus 25¢ delivery per book and applicable sales tax, if any*. In Canada, bill me at the bargain price of $3.25 plus 25¢ delivery per book and applicable taxes**. That's the complete price and a savings of at least 10% off the cover prices—what a great deal! I understand that accepting the 2 free books and gift places me under no obligation ever to buy any books. I can always return a shipment and cancel at any time. Even if I never buy another book from Silhouette, the 2 free books and gift are mine to keep forever. So why not take us up on our invitation. You'll be glad you did!

215 SEN C24Q
315 SEN C24R

Name	(PLEASE PRINT)	
Address	Apt.#	
City	State/Prov.	Zip/Postal Code

* Terms and prices subject to change without notice. Sales tax applicable in N.Y.
** Canadian residents will be charged applicable provincial taxes and GST.
 All orders subject to approval. Offer limited to one per household.
 ® are registered trademarks of Harlequin Enterprises Limited.

SROM00_R   ©1998 Harlequin Enterprises Limited

Look Who's Celebrating Our 20ᵗʰ Anniversary:

Celebrate **20** YEARS

"Happy 20ᵗʰ birthday, Silhouette. You made the writing dream of hundreds of women a reality. You enabled us to give [women] the stories [they] wanted to read and helped us teach [them] about the power of love."

—*New York Times* bestselling author
Debbie Macomber

"I wish you continued success, Silhouette Books.... Thank you for giving me a chance to do what I love best in all the world."

—International bestselling author
Diana Palmer

"A visit to Silhouette is a guaranteed happy ending, a chance to touch magic for a little while.... It refreshes and revitalizes and makes us feel better.... I hope Silhouette goes on forever."

—Award-winning bestselling author
Marie Ferrarella

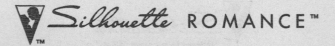

Silhouette ROMANCE ™